PACIFIC

PACIFIC

A Novel

Tom Drury

Grove Press
New York

Permission for lyrics from "Fake Empire" by The National was granted by PostHoc Management.

Published simultaneously in Canada
Printed in the United States of America

FIRST EDITION

ISBN-13: 978-0-8021-1999-5

Grove Press
an imprint of Grove/Atlantic, Inc.
841 Broadway
New York, NY 10003

Distributed by Publishers Group West

www.groveatlantic.com

13 14 15 16   10 9 8 7 6 5 4 3 2 1

To Christian

Then the four of them went to another city.

"What craft shall we take on?" said Pryderi.

"We will make shields," said Manawydan.

"Do we know anything about that?" said Pryderi.

"We will attempt it," he said.

The Mabinogion

PACIFIC

CHAPTER ONE

TINY AND Micah sat on the back porch of the house where they lived outside the town of Boris, watching the sun go down behind the train tracks and the trees.

"Say you're carrying something," said Tiny.

"Yeah? Like what?" Fourteen years old, Micah wore a forest-green stocking hat. His hair curved like feathers around his calm brown eyes.

"Something of value," said Tiny. "This ashtray here. Say this ashtray is of value."

The ashtray was made of green glass with yellowed seashells glued to the rim. Likely it came from Yellowstone or some other tourist place originally. It might have *been* of value. Micah picked it up and walked to the end of the porch and back.

"Good," said Tiny. "Something of value you carry in front of you and never at your side."

"I just didn't want the ashes to fall out."

"Now say you get in a fight."

"Yeah, I'm not doing that."

"What you do is put your head down and ram them in the solar plexus. It's unexpected."

"I wouldn't expect it."

"Well, no one does," said Tiny. "Sometimes they faint. They almost always fall over."

"Got it."

"And never, never get a credit card."

"How would I pay it back?"

"You wouldn't. That's the idea."

It was a cool night in May. The red sky shaded the grass and the shed and the house.

"Do you still want to go?" said Tiny. "You can change your mind any time."

"Dad, I've never been in an airplane."

"We could get Paul Francis to take you up."

"I mean a real airplane."

Tiny nodded. "I just said that to be saying something."

A band-tailed Cooper's hawk came from the west and landed on a hardwood branch with new leaves.

"There's your hawk," said Tiny. "Come to say goodbye."

Dan Norman walked out of his house carrying the pieces of a broken table. He and Louise still lived on the old Klar farm on the hill.

The table had fallen apart in the living room. It was not bearing unusual weight and neither Dan nor Louise was nearby when it fell. Just the table's time, apparently.

A car pulled slowly into the driveway and a woman got out and stood in the yellow circle of the yard light. She had long blond hair, wore a pleated red dress and white gloves.

"You don't remember me," she said.

"I do," said Dan. "Joan Gower."

He shifted the table pieces over to his left arm and they shook hands.

"Did you know we get second chances, Sheriff?" said Joan.

"Sometimes. I'd say I knew that."

"He will turn again and have compassion upon us and subdue our iniquities."

"I'm not sheriff anymore, though."

The door of the house opened and Louise came out wearing a long white button-down shirt as a dress.

"Who are you talking to?"

"Joan Gower."

"Really."

Louise had tangled red hair, wild and alive with the light of the house behind her.

"Is this business?"

"I'm getting my son back," said Joan.

"Give me those, love," said Louise.

She took the table parts from Dan and headed for the hedge behind the house.

Louise put the wood in the trash burner and went on to the barn, the dust of the old farmyard cool and powdery on her feet.

Empty and dark as a church, the barn was no longer used for anything. Louise climbed the ladder and walked across the floor of the hayloft.

The planks had been worn smooth by decades of boots and bales and the changing of seasons. She sat in the open door, dangled her bare legs over the side, lit a cigarette, and smoked in the night.

Dan and Joan were down there, talking in the yard. Louise listened to the quiet sound of their voices. What they were saying she could not tell.

She saw Joan reach up and put her hand on Dan's shoulder, and then his face. The gesture made Louise happy for some reason.

Maybe that it was beautiful. A graceful sight to be seen in the country, whatever else you might think of it.

Lyris and Albert slouched on a davenport smoking grass from a wooden pipe from El Salvador and reading the promotional copy printed on Lyris's moving boxes.

Lyris was Joan's other child—Micah's half sister, Tiny's stepdaughter. At twenty-three she had just moved in with her boyfriend, Albert Robeshaw.

The boxes were said to be good for four moves or twelve years' storage, and anyone who got more use out of them was directed to sign on to the company's website and explain.

"As if anyone would do that," said Albert.

"To whom it may concern," said Lyris.

"We move constantly."

"We love your boxes."

"So what are we doing?" said Albert.

"About what?"

"Are we going to see Micah?"

Lyris drew on the pipe. "The little scamper," she said.

Joan had given Lyris up for adoption at birth. She appeared at Joan and Tiny's door when she was sixteen and Micah seven. When Joan went away Lyris raised Micah as much as anyone did.

Louise came down from the hayloft and walked back to the house. Dan made her a drink and opened a beer, and they faced each other across the kitchen table.

"What have we learned?"

Dan raised his eyebrows. "Sounds like Micah Darling's going to live with her in California."

"What's it got to do with us?"

"I think she just wanted to tell someone."

"I saw her touch you," said Louise.

"Did you?"

Louise picked up the bottle cap from the beer and flicked it at Dan.

"Yeah, man. Pretty sweet scene."

Dan caught the cap and tossed it toward the corner, where it landed on the floor by the wastebasket.

"Where were you?" said Dan.

"Up in the barn."

"How was it?"

"The same. Good."

*   *   *

When Lyris and Albert arrived, Tiny was drinking vodka and Hi-C and watching the Ironman Triathlon on television. An athlete had completed the running part and was staggering around like a newborn colt. People tried to corral him, with little success.

"What you need in that situation is a wheelbarrow," said Tiny.

Lyris and Albert stood on either side of his chair, looking at the screen.

"Is there archery in this?" Albert asked.

Tiny laughed. "Hell no, there isn't archery. You swim, ride a bike, and run. It all has to be done in seventeen minutes."

"That can't be right," said Lyris.

"I'm sorry. Hours," said Tiny.

"Where's Micah?"

Tiny tipped his head back to gaze at the ceiling. "In his room. Packing his belongings."

"How are you?"

"I'm all right."

Albert sat down in a chair to watch TV, or watch Tiny watching TV. Lyris climbed the narrow stairs between pineboard walls lined with pictures that she had cut from magazines and framed.

Micah had Lyris's old suitcase open on his bed and was folding clothes into it. The suitcase was made of woven sand-colored fibers with red metal corners. From the pocket of her jeans Lyris took a folded sheet of paper and tucked it in the suitcase.

"Okay, boy, that's my number," she said. "You get into trouble, you need to talk, I'm here."

"Who will call me 'boy' in California?"

"No one. That's why you shouldn't leave."

"Do you think so?"

She shrugged. "Go and see what it is."

"Are airplanes loud?"

"You get used to it," said Lyris. "Sometimes they kind of shake."

"They shake?"

"Well, no. Rattle. Occasionally. From bumps in the clouds. But that's nothing. If you get nervous just look at the flight people. No matter what happens, they always seem to be thinking, Hmm-hmm-hmm, wonder what I'll have for supper tonight."

The hotel that Joan stayed in had a tavern with blue neon lights in the windows. She went in and sat at the bar and ordered a Dark and Stormy.

The bartender was a young woman in a black and white smock with horizontal ivy vines above the belt and black-eyed Susans below.

"Are you here for the wedding?" she asked.

Joan explained about Micah—how she'd left him seven years ago and wanted a chance to make up for it.

"Oh my," said the bartender. "That will be quite a change for everyone."

"It will," said Joan. "They all probably think it will be a big disaster."

"Well, it seems brave to me."

Joan took a drink. "It does?"

"Oh, yeah. Even kind of, what would you say, inspirational."

"You are the sweetest girl," said Joan.

"You look like someone on TV."

"I am."

"Sister Mia. On *Forensic Mystic*."

Joan nodded.

"Oh my gosh," said the bartender. "Would you autograph my hand?"

"I would be honored."

"Say 'Sister Mia.'"

Joan held the bartender's hand palm up and using a purple felt pen wrote "Sister Mia" and drew a heart with an arrow through it.

"People will think I did this myself," said the bartender.

"Why would you?"

Joan finished her drink and went to her room. It was on the second floor in the back, overlooking a pond with dark trees and houses all around. She turned off the lights in the room and stood on the balcony looking at the water.

Tiny made breakfast and Micah came downstairs to the smell of scrambled eggs and Canadian bacon and coffee. They ate and Micah asked Tiny if he was going to fight with Joan and Tiny shook his head.

"I don't think about her that much anymore."

"You watch her show."

"Sometimes."

"You must think of her then."

Tiny put pepper on his food from a red tin. "I have trouble enough following the story."

"I believe that."

"You have to mind her," said Tiny. "Maybe you think she owes you. That won't work. You have to mind her like you mind me."

"I don't mind you."

"Well, use your imagination."

"You seem more like a brother than a father to me," said Micah. "And I don't mean that bad."

Tiny got up and carried his plate and silverware to the sink, where he washed and rinsed them and put them on the drainboard.

"I don't take it bad," he said.

Joan arrived in the middle of the morning, and Micah watched her from the window. She crossed the yard smiling, as if thinking it was not so different from what she remembered.

The three of them met on the front porch. For a moment they seemed to be waiting for someone to appear who could tell them what to do.

Then Joan took Micah in her arms and pressed her head to his chest. He was a head taller than she.

"I can hear your heart," she said.

"Come on inside," said Tiny.

"You have to invite me."

"I just did."

"Come in, Mom," said Micah.

Joan took a chair at the table. Her eyelids and lips were brushed with fine reddish powder, and her skin glowed like a lamp in the room.

"We had eggs and Canadian bacon," said Tiny. "Do you want some?"

"No thank you, I ate at the hotel," she said quietly.

"How was it?"

"Fair."

"Where you staying?"

"The American Suites," said Joan.

"Nice."

"Oh! There's the broom."

"What?" said Tiny.

"I see the broom. I bought it, and now I'm looking right at it."

"Yeah, we haven't changed. It's missing a few straws."

Micah went upstairs to have a last look at his room. He thought he should feel sad, but he only wondered when he would see it again. Would he be different then? Who would he be?

"And how is the plumbing business going?" said Joan.

Tiny explained how he lost the plumbing business. The pipes had burst in a house, and the house froze and fell in on itself. The insurance company came in and sued all the contractors.

"Was it your fault?"

"Any pipe you let freeze with water in it, that pipe'll split. Who puts it in is immaterial. Could be Jesus, pipe's going to break. Since then I've been moving things for people."

"Do you need money?"

With his hands on the table, Tiny pushed his chair back and looked at her. "I have nothing against you. You want to do things for Micah, and I hope you can. But do I want money? Come on, Joan."

"I'm sorry."

"This is my house."

"I know it."

She apologized again, and he waved a hand as if to say it was done.

"You want to stay over? You can have Lyris's old room."

"We fly out of Stone City this afternoon," said Joan. "Is she going to be here?"

"Her and Albert Robeshaw came over last night. She's still kind of mad at you."

"You can't blame her," said Joan.

"Oh, probably not."

Tiny's mother arrived, her silhouette looming in the doorway. She yelled hello though Tiny and Joan were sitting right there for anyone to see.

She wore a large Hawaiian shirt, jeans with hammer loops, and Red Wing boots. People feared her, as if she had special powers, but she was just an old lady given to yelling at people and playing with their minds.

Joan stood and gave her a hug, which made her uncomfortable. It wasn't that she didn't like Joan, she just wasn't used to being hugged.

Micah walked down the stairs sideways, dragging Lyris's suitcase by its red plastic handle. The suitcase bumped down the stairs. The kitchen became crowded, and Tiny took the suitcase and led everyone out to the front yard. They gathered around Micah in the shadow of the willow tree.

"I'm going to miss you," said Micah's grandmother. "But you'll be all right. There'll be somebody there to help you when you run into trouble."

"I will," said Joan.

"Besides you. There's someone else."

Tiny stood behind his mother, gazing absently into the panoramic view of her Hawaiian shirt. Her predictions never sur-
prised him. She made lots of them. He hoped this one would
come true.

The shirt was dark blue and green and depicted nightfall in an
island village of palm trees and grass huts with yellow lights burning
in the windows. A pretty place.

Then Micah put thumb and finger to the corners of his mouth
and whistled. Pretty soon an old doe goat crept around the side of
the house. Micah and Lyris had raised her together.

The goat came soft-footed down the grass. The reds and whites
of her coat had faded to shades of silver. She surveyed the visitors
and then stared at Micah, as if to say, Oh, wait a minute. You're
leaving? That's what this is all about?

Micah fell to his knees and roughed up the goat's long and matted
coat. You could see him trying not to cry, but he did anyway. The
goat stared with slotted eyes at the road that went by the house.

"This is harder than I thought it would be," said Micah.

Tiny and his mother stood in the yard, watching Joan's car go
around the bend. A bank of blue and gray clouds moved in, hiding the sun. Colette took out a pipe and a pouch of tobacco and
proceeded to smoke.

"And then there was one," she said.

"Looking that way," said Tiny softly.

"You think he's doing the right thing?"

"He might be."

She walked off to her truck, and Tiny went into the house, closed
the door, and walked up the stairs with his shoulders bumping the
walls. Micah's bed was made with a blanket of red and black plaid
and a light blue pillow centered beneath the headboard. A hockey
stick leaned in the corner, blade wrapped in frayed electrical tape,
near an old poster from a movie about heroic dogs.

The bedsprings wheezed like an accordion as Tiny sat down at the foot of the bed. A car went by, the road became quiet, and light rain began to fall against the window.

He sat with his forearms on his knees and his hands folded, remembering when the goat was young, how she and Micah would dance around the yard.

Chapter Two

S INCE DECLINING to run for a sixth term as sheriff, Dan Norman worked for a private detective agency on the sixth floor of the Orange Building in Stone City.

The agency was called Lord Norman Associates, after its founder, Lynn Lord, but Dan and his assistant, Donna, did most of the work.

Lynn Lord had more or less retired to the basement of his house, where he designed and built clandestine audio and video devices, some of which had been patented. Lynn was said to be one of the best darts players in the county, not that the county was teeming with darts players.

One day a middle-aged couple came in to see Dan. Their case would turn out to be important, though not in a way that anyone could have predicted.

"Do you have children?" said the man.

"No," said Dan.

"Well, then you don't know."

They explained in halting fashion, correcting and annotating each other's remarks. Couples rarely speak smoothly to a private investigator. Anyway, their daughter, Wendy, had fallen in with a man from out of town. Jack Snow was his name, and he ran a mail-order trade in Celtic artifacts from a warehouse by the railyards. He'd moved in with Wendy, and she kept the books for his business. Before that, she had made beaded moccasins of her own design.

"Now, when you say artifacts," said Dan.

"We haven't seen them," said the woman. "Haven't been allowed to. But we think they're worthless."

"Why?"

"Certain things she said."

"'They're not what they seem,'" said the father.

"Meaning what?"

"She wouldn't elaborate," said the mother. "She said we were down on her boyfriend, and our concerns were trite."

"Aren't all antiques overpriced?" said Dan.

"What if they're not antiques," said the mother.

"He's raking in the money," said the father. "They're riding around town in a Shelby Mustang. One weekend they up and flew to Reno to play blackjack. It doesn't feel right."

"We don't want Wendy mixed up in anything."

"Maybe we're crazy," said the father.

"We hope we are."

As they spoke, Dan took notes on a legal pad:

    daughter
    Wendy
    boyfriend
    Jack Snow
    artifacts
    warehouse
    not what they seem
    Shelby
    Reno
    crazy

Louise drove a bleached-blue IH Scout II with a three-speed manual on the column. It was a rough ride but that was okay because she liked feeling the road. The door seals were dry and cracked. The smells of springtime drifted in: new grass, pollen, bird wings.

She had inherited the three-story Kleeborg Building in Stone City and ran a thrift store on the ground floor and rented out the rest as apartments.

Louise and the man who left her the building, Perry Kleeborg, had been in the photography business together, and after he died, in his nineties, she didn't want to keep it going without him.

Over time the thrift store filled up with the things left by the emptying of the old farmhouses. Small chairs of coarse fabric, barometers and birdcages, hunting jackets lined with flannel, books bound in dark green and red, pottery from the old studios.

Louise would buy things from the forties, fifties, and sixties, but nothing from the seventies and after, for that was when the quality fell off. The hours she kept were noon to nine.

That morning, before opening, she sat out front with coffee and a smoke. She wore a man's pinstriped jacket and watched the traffic along the street. The sun was out, and she felt good and warm with the wind blowing her hair.

A crow spiraled down between the blocks as a white and blue transit bus came from the east. The crown of the bus clipped the crow and left it flapping on the pavement.

Louise ran into the street, took off her jacket, and used it to gather up the crow. She carried it into the store and put it in a cardboard box. The bird had black eyes ringed with gold and bobbed its head in disbelief, to be one moment flying and the next in a box.

The lining of the jacket was streaked with crow liquid of some kind, and Louise took the jacket out behind the shop and put it in the dumpster.

When she returned, she had a customer—tall and thin and pale, perhaps in her twenties, dressed in black, with shining white hair and inch-long bangs.

"My name is Sandra Zulma," she said. "I'm looking for a rock." She pressed her fists together to indicate the size.

"We have a geode," said Louise. "You can see the crystals inside. On the table with the coin banks of the presidents."

"No. It's a . . . particular rock."

"Is it special?"

The woman looked at Louise with clear blue eyes. "Some say it's a piece of the Lia Fáil. Or it might be the stone thrown by Cúchulainn to keep Conall's chariot from following him to Loch Echtra. Or a cairn stone left by the raiders of the Inn at Leinster."

"Gee," said Louise. "I doubt we'd get anything like that here."

Then they heard the sound of scratching.

"What's that?" said the customer.

"It's a crow that got hit by a bus."

"Can I see?"

Louise opened the box, and Sandra Zulma knelt and reached inside, setting the crow upright. When she withdrew her hands it lay down again.

"The raven, the blood, and the snow," she said.

"Mmm," said Louise. "I hope you find your rock."

"I'm at the Continental Hotel if it turns up."

After she left, Louise locked the store and took the crow across town to twin veterinarians she knew. They examined the bird on a high table of stainless steel, spreading one wing and then the other. They seemed happy to have a bird to work on instead of dogs, cats, and livestock all the time.

Business turned profitable later in the day. Louise sold an ominous cabinet that had been in the shop forever, a set of cocktail glasses decorated with pinup girls, a bait-casting reel, and a sun-faded series of Zane Grey novels, including an autographed copy of *Wanderer of the Wasteland*.

Louise could tell that the book buyer hoped she wouldn't know the value of the set, but she held fast and got a good price.

Lyris and Albert lived in an apartment on the top floor of the Kleeborg Building, and one evening Lyris stopped into the shop after work. She was a clerk for the gravestone salesman Don Gary, who had an office by the cemetery on the east side of Stone City.

Lyris was an uncertain shopper who crept through the aisles, as if every hat rack, wringer washer, and abandoned golf club required intense consideration.

And so Louise showed her one of the better things in the shop, a large oil painting of men and horses stopping at a mountain pass in Tibet. The men smoked a long-stemmed pipe, and the horses stood nearby wearing sashes of yellow and green.

Lyris said it was the most beautiful painting she had ever seen and asked the price.

"It's free," said Louise. "A present for your new apartment."

Then Louise and Lyris settled into a paisley sofa with funhouse springs and they drank glasses of wine and rested their feet on crates that had long ago held California tangerines.

"Dan and I think the world of Albert," said Louise.

"How long have you known him?"

"Well, how long *have* we? Since he was in high school anyway."

"What was he like?"

"Like he is now, maybe a little funnier. He played guitar in a band."

"His job takes it out of him," said Lyris.

Albert wrote for the Stone City newspaper, known for being shorthanded and for having dropped the cartoon strip *Blondie*, to much disapproval.

"Have you met his family?"

"Some of them. There's so many."

The Robeshaws were among the more prosperous farming families in the county. They owned five places, raising corn and beans and hogs, some cattle, and a horse or two, and Albert was the youngest of the six children.

"They're very competitive," said Louise. "One night I got to see them play Scrabble. Not something I would care to watch again."

Louise refilled their glasses, thinking that she must sound like her own mother, who in the old days would instruct her on the ways and faults of the community. But Louise was not Lyris's mother, though she might have been, given the difference in their ages.

A pair of white leather gloves were on an end table by the sofa, and Lyris put them on and spread her fingers wide.

"You work for the tombstone guy," said Louise.

"Yeah."

"How is that?"

"He's hyperactive. Puts on Aqua Velva at work."

"He does not."

Lyris raised her chin, patting cheeks and neck with her gloved hands.

"Like this. It makes a cloud in the air. I guess it takes people's minds off their grief maybe. And sometimes, when he's walking around a corner, he moves his hands like he's turning a steering wheel."

Louise laughed with surprise in her heart and put her arm around Lyris's shoulders.

Then, thinking she'd been too familiar, she drew her arm back until it rested awkwardly in the deep space between the cushion and the back of the sofa. What the fuck is wrong with this couch? she wondered.

"I'm glad Albert found you," she said. "He needed someone. You'll be good for each other."

Lyris took the gloves off and laid them on the table, pressing them flat with the edge of her hand. "I don't know."

"Well, you don't. That's all right."

"I get afraid sometimes."

"Of what?"

"Oh, that I will be left, or that it's the end of the world."

"Yeah," said Louise. "Yeah."

"It happens at night. I wake up and I don't know where I am. I cry out."

Louise freed her arm from the sofa. "You're in a new place, with a new boyfriend."

"I scream, actually. I just say 'cry out' because it sounds prettier. 'She cried out, in her sleep.'"

"But Albert's there."

"Yes. But I think he'll get tired of it, don't you? This terrified thing in his bed."

Lyris had green eyes that looked in slightly different directions, as if watching for trouble that might come from anywhere. They glassed over as she stared at the goods in the shop.

"It's all right to cry if you need to," said Louise.

The girl nodded, looking miserable. "Ah yeah, I think I do."

And so she cried, with rapid breaths and big round tears rolling from the corners of her eyes.

Louise held her, petting her hair. "Rough old world," she said. "I know it."

After a while Lyris sat back and dried her face with her hands. She laughed a little, as one does after an unexpected cry.

"I think I got your shirt wet," she said.

"It's only a thing," said Louise.

She and Lyris carried the painting of the men and horses in the mountain pass up the linoleum stairs. The apartment was a decent place. Everything was old but it all worked. Louise looked around at the boxes and the tall windows and the dark wood floors, and she thought of other things that would go well in this place.

The phone rang as Louise was turning off the lights in the shop. The twin veterinarians got on the speakerphone to give her the bad news: the crow had died of internal injuries.

"Oh, really?" she said unsteadily. "He was doing so good, I thought. I was really counting on him getting better for some reason. . . . Yeah. . . . No. . . . I understand. Goodbye."

Louise was sadder than the death of a crow would otherwise make her. She'd begun a story about saving the bird, the story had come to a different ending, and she could not change it.

Chapter Three

Coming into Los Angeles, where jet airplanes crossed the mountains and drifted down over rivers of cars and trucks, Micah could not imagine people and things enough to fill the buildings he saw. It was the world's largest place.

Joan had a silver Audi with a straight stick and the roundness and precision of a toy. She wore big, dark sunglasses and drove with a thoughtless confidence Micah did not remember. She knew the way without thinking, turning down a curving, single-lane highway high in the sky.

Micah saw a giant woman dressed in an emerald gown and holding a violin on the side of a parking garage, and he saw the shining towers above the highways, and he thought maybe he'd made a mistake, which made everything more interesting.

Joan lived in a village north of Los Angeles with her husband and her husband's son. The husband's name was Rob Hammerhill, and he produced animal shows on television and managed a library of wildlife footage. His business took him often to Russia.

The house was a cluster of reddish boxes hidden from the road by vines, orange trees, and evergreens. No one was home. Joan led Micah to a room on the second floor in the back. Everything was new: bed and desk, wicker laundry hamper, big chair of blue and white stripe, bedside table with a black box on it. The smell of fresh paint made him miss the grounding smells of home—tobacco, motor oil, gravel dust, things like that.

Joan raised the window shade, and they looked out at a slate terrace, deep green yard, and, beyond that, stone steps climbing a hillside rife with trees and bushes and ivy.

"This is your room," said Joan. "I hope you like it, though you might not at first. That's okay. I want you to feel free to tell me what you think."

"It's nice."

"Those are redwood trees," said Joan. "Thank you for letting me be your mom again."

When Joan left the room, Micah opened his suitcase and dug out a framed photograph of Tiny and Lyris. They were washing the goat in a wading pool, and the goat looked into the camera, wondering if it could be eaten.

Micah set the picture on the desk, lowered the shade, and lay on the bed. He looked at the black box and pressed the top of it, and it made the sound of rain. Then he pressed it again: the singing of birds. He cycled through wind, crickets, ocean waves, rain again, and he fell asleep.

Someone said it was morning time, and Micah opened his eyes.

"I lied," said a boy in the room. He was older than Micah, small and thin with a dark goatee. "It's evening time."

Micah sat up and looked around for his shoes, before realizing they were on his feet.

"I'm Eamon," said the boy. "We're the sons of the people in the house, so we have to get along, no matter if we hate each other or what."

"What time is it?"

"Seven-thirty."

Micah yawned. "I'm Micah. Nice to meet you."

"Are you a loner?"

"Don't think so."

"Good. Let's go for a drive."

Soon they were on another freeway. The green banks of the hills came down to the road and rose again on the other side. They listened to a band Eamon liked called the Libation Bearers.

The hilltops looked close in the evening light and Micah thought you could climb them and look around, though it would probably take longer than it appeared.

"How was the flight?" said Eamon.

"I got patted down in Minneapolis."

"You look dangerous."

"I'm sure."

"One time they dusted my backpack. I was seven years old. It's an honor, really."

They drove for half an hour and got off the highway, headed south on a two-lane road that wound through tunnels and canyons. Micah rolled down the window, feeling the cool wind on his face.

It was forested country, and they arrived at last on a soft dirt lane, beneath the interwoven branches of trees, with horse farms on either side, or perhaps it was the same farm.

"We're meeting some friends of mine," said Eamon. "How do you feel about drugs?"

"I've done grass," said Micah.

"We say 'weed.' Interesting."

"Well, we say 'weed' too. I don't know why I said 'grass.'"

"Six of one."

"It didn't do anything. I thought I was smoking it wrong."

"It's not all good."

Eamon led Micah down a grass path between white wooden fences. A few horses stood stoic in the pastures and others could be heard knocking about in stalls. A husky with white eyes barked in a friendly way and lay down panting.

The three friends of Eamon sat peacefully on the front steps of a little house. With crescent eyes and thick black braids, Charlotte

looked like one of the girls in the Boston Persuasion shoe com-
mercials. Thea's small face shone in the twilight. Curtis's hair lay
dense across his forehead, the color of wheat.

"This is my stepbrother Micah," said Eamon. "Son of Joan
Gower."

"And Tiny Darling," said Micah.

"Your father's name is Tiny Darling?" said Thea. "That's fantastic."

"Well, his name is Charles, really," said Micah modestly. "Only
my mom called him that."

"Micah's from the Middle West," said Eamon.

Charlotte was wearing multicolored necklaces of glass beads, and
she took one off and put it on Micah.

"Welcome to Southern California," she said.

They walked beside the house and made themselves comfortable in
lawn chairs. Curtis had a backpack, from which he took a translucent
red bong, a gallon of distilled water, and a glassine bag of dried leaves.

"This strain is called King Scout," he said. "It's a short high and
kind of intense. It grows on the sides of mountains in a cool climate.
Very hard to get."

"We're not the drug culture," said Charlotte. "Cocaine we would
never do. Meth we would never do."

"Vision drugs, as opposed to metabolism drugs," said Thea, and
the others agreed.

"You don't have to, Micah," said Eamon.

"They say you can do old drugs with new people, and new drugs
with old people, but not new drugs with new people," said Thea.

Curtis prepared the bong. "It's not one size fits all," he said. "You
shouldn't enter into it with fear. That I agree with."

"I'm not afraid," said Micah.

"I'll be his copilot," said Charlotte.

Joan and Rob had a late supper at a restaurant on West Sunset. She
had the Caesar salad, and he had macaroni and cheese baked in a
ceramic dish, and they split a bottle of wine.

The soft orange lighting and sexy pictures on the wall made Joan think of sex. She imagined the people in the pictures coming to life after closing time, drifting down to get it on.

"What are you thinking about?" said Rob.

"I'm going to audition for a movie," said Joan. "It's called *The Powder Horn,* about Davy Crockett."

"What's the part?"

"Ann Flowers."

"Who's she?"

"When Davy Crockett was fifteen, he made this canoe trip across a river in a winter storm, because no ferryman would take him. His boat was swamped, and he was freezing, and when he did get across he had to walk three miles before he found a house. Ann Flowers is the daughter of that house. The canoe story is true, but Ann is made up. So they gave him some liquor to warm him up, and he and Ann Flowers ended up sharing a bed."

"With all that follows."

"No. That's what's different. They just lie on their sides looking at each other, far into the night."

"How old is she?"

"His age. Somebody else will play her then."

"Where do you come in?"

"Thirty some years go by, right? Davy Crockett gets into politics, wins, loses, goes to the Alamo, all the things he does. And after the Alamo he shows up at Ann Flowers's cabin, and they spend the night together again. It's bittersweet, because their lives have gone by, and in the morning he's gone."

"The older role can be the better one," said Rob. "But I thought Davy Crockett died at the Alamo."

"He did. It's his spirit that visits Ann, but she doesn't know that till he's gone. A friend says, Hey, did you hear what happened at the Alamo? So now she doesn't know what to think, having slept with a ghost or whatever he was. And when she goes back to her little cabin, what do you think she finds?"

"A powder horn."

"Yes. And 'clutches to breast' and up music and roll credits."

"And this is getting made?"

"They've got financing," said Joan. "They just need a bridge loan. Or a mezzanine loan. Some kind of loan that sounds like architecture. I was thinking I would get into movies so I would have more time for Micah."

"Where is he?"

"Eamon took him to see Charlotte Mann's horse."

Rob waved for the check. "What is a powder horn?"

"I'm not entirely sure."

A transparent blue screen had unscrolled before Micah's eyes. The screen was cracked like a mosaic, with beads of light pulsing along infinite pathways. On the other side of all this disturbance were his new friends, small and geometrical in appearance.

Then Micah looked at the sky and found that the stars were connected by the lines in the screen, as if he had been born and brought here to make this discovery.

"Is it happening?" said Charlotte.

"There are lines between the stars," said Micah.

"Are you okay? Look at me."

Charlotte leaned close. Her forehead was damp, and he reached out to brush back a lock of hair that had escaped her braids.

"You have perfect eyebrows," he said. "I wish I had a mirror so I could show you."

She closed her eyes, and with the tip of her finger she wiped her eyelids dry, first one, then the other.

"Once I saw a man on a street corner," she said. "At La Brea and Third. He had his little boy on his back in a carrier. And the boy had wooden train cars, one in each hand, and he was driving them around on his father's shoulders as they walked."

Eamon shuffled around in the dust, looking at his bare feet, with a shoe on each hand. "I got a lemon one time and it had a phone number on it," he said. "So I called the number and this lady answered and I asked why her phone number was written on a lemon, and she said it shouldn't be, I should just throw the lemon away and forget I ever saw it. So I said I would and in a few minutes she called back and asked where I was going to throw it away, and I said what, and she said the lemon, and I said probably a trash can, and she said that wasn't good, because someone might see it and think here is a perfectly good lemon going to waste and they might pick it up and call her like I did. So I said well where do you want me to throw it and she thought for a minute and said where are you now, and I told her I was on Franklin by the Magic Castle and she said don't go anywhere, so I waited and in about twenty minutes this little green Lotus pulls up and the woman rolled the window down and she said do you have the lemon and I said yeah and gave it to her and she gave me twenty dollars and drove away."

They laughed. The dog began to bark, and a noise came down from the sky. A helicopter flew sideways over the hills, its light coming and going, a pure silvery beam touching the ground, as if the helicopter were walking on stilts.

"What's that about?" said Micah.

"No one really knows," said Curtis.

"I used to think they were looking for criminals," said Thea. "But they do it so often that I don't think that anymore."

"Maybe they're bored," said Eamon. "Just fucking around till quitting time."

"They're like the night watchman in a Russian story," said Charlotte. "Checking the doors of the midnight village to make sure they're locked."

"I lived in that village," said Micah.

Then a man in corduroy jacket and white cowboy hat rode down from the stables in a golf cart, the husky and two yellow Labs trotting behind. The dogs found them first and licked their faces while the man stopped the golf cart.

"That's Angel," whispered Charlotte to Micah. "The owner."

"What's going on here?" he said. "I have the television on, and I can hear the noise you're making all the way up the hill."

"We're sorry, Angel," said Charlotte. "We'll be quiet. We're leaving now."

The driver of the golf cart looked at each of them in turn, touched the brim of his hat, turned the cart around, and drove back to the stables, escorted by the dogs.

"Now Angel's mad at me," said Charlotte.

"I want that golf cart," said Thea.

From the horse farm, they went to the beach in Santa Monica, where they bought hamburgers and french fries and sat on a blanket on the sand, eating and listening to the sound of the ocean.

When Micah got home he hung the beads Charlotte had given him on the photograph of Tiny, Lyris, and the goat.

The next day Joan was at an auto salvage yard off Mission Road shooting *Forensic Mystic*. Most of the autos seemed beyond salvaging. They were twisted and sliced, mangled and melted, and the yard workers had stacked them into neat mounds like city blocks with paths running between.

The yard made the highway system seem like the work of an evil god. Joan sat in a mallard-green canvas chair beneath a parasol.

In this scene she would throw away a knife that had been used in a murder. Her character, Sister Mia, would debate whether to turn it in to the police. That was her conflict. Everyone must have an arc and a conflict.

Joan strolled the junkyard path, slapping the knife blade on her thigh. An athletic brunette walked backward, Steadicam strapped on her body. Then they laid dolly tracks and filmed Joan's walk from the side.

She flung knife after knife into a mountain of wrecked cars. The prop master had knives to spare. Joan wondered if archaeologists would find the knives someday and deduce that people had fought over the cars.

At lunchtime she got an orange from the food tables and walked to the fringe of the salvage yard, where she could see the Los Angeles River and the skyline across the way.

She held the orange in her hands, tearing the rind with her teeth. A dark ribbon of water moved slowly down the trough of the riverbed. She thought she would soon be written out of the show.

The knife toss was Joan's last scene of the day. She drove home and made lunch for Micah, who was just getting up. He sat at the dining room table, head wet from the shower, scratching his arms.

"How were the horses?" said Joan.

"We didn't get to see them. We had to leave the farm because we were laughing too much."

"Well, at least you had a good time."

"Then we went to the ocean."

"What did you think?"

Micah took a bite of the sandwich Joan had made. "It felt like I belonged there," he said.

She came over and touched his wet hair. "Doesn't it? I know just what you mean. Though I worried when you were out so late."

"You don't have to, Mom. I'm not seven anymore."

"I know you're not," said Joan.

It was true in some ways—she'd forgotten that he was alive all this time and not waiting for her to return to begin again.

"You don't know what it's like," she said.

"Because you left?"

"It must have seemed selfish."

"I thought you were in trouble," said Micah. "I didn't think that it was something you did to someone."

"To you," said Joan. "That's who it was done to."

"Sometimes I pretended you broke the law and didn't want to bring it down on us. Like you robbed a bank or something."

Joan laughed. "I should have."

"You wore a blue bandanna to hide your face and the newspapers called you the Blue Bandit. All the bank tellers were afraid that you might be heading their way."

"Oh Micah," said Joan. "I hope I haven't hurt you too much."

She felt good to be reminded of the little boy he had been. He seemed real to her for the first time since she'd seen him again in the doorway of Tiny's house.

Joan went to North Hollywood to read for the role of the older Ann Flowers in *The Powder Horn*. Five men sat on one side of a table, and Joan stood on the other, with a brass bed and chair on her side of the room.

"We love what you're doing in *Mystic Forensic*," said the director.

"*Forensic Mystic*," said Joan.

"Of course."

"Everyone does that."

"We'd like to go over the scene in the cabin. Do you need a script?"

"I know the part."

"Night. Crockett knocks, you rise, you open door. And the line is yours."

"Good evening," said Joan.

An associate producer read Davy Crockett's lines.

"Evening, miss."

"Are you lost?"

"Yes, that sounds accurate. I crossed the New River in a storm. They said wait for the ferryman but I wouldn't listen."

"The New River is two hundred miles from here."

"It might be another time I'm thinking of."

"David?"

"And you're Ann."

"Come in, man. Get by the fire."

"I could use whiskey if you got it."

"This is as it was before."

"You're hardly any older, Ann. I can still see those eyes under the rafters."

"Why have you come?"

"I don't know. I thought that I would get out all right because, you know, that's what I do. But I'm nothing now."

"You're here."

"In a manner. Did you get married, Ann? Have a family and all?"

"I never did. I suppose I had my suitors. But that night, when you came to our place, you were so cold. Just a boy. It got into my heart somehow. And kind of stayed there."

"That must be it."

"Must be what?"

"Why here. Why you."

"Hush, David. Drink your drink. We have all night for talking."

Joan was in tears. She never had trouble finding the emotions in the words.

"I don't know what to say," said the director.

"Now, there is some nudity," said the associate producer.

"I know."

"Could you undress?"

Joan stepped out of her shoes, unbuttoned her dress, slipped it off her shoulders, and let it fall. She raised her arms, hands cupped as if holding mourning doves that would fly away on violet wings.

They were writing notes. "Now Joan, if you could lie on the bed?"

Of course. The bed wasn't there for the fun of it. She crossed the room and lay down, closed her eyes, and pretended she heard rain on rooftops.

She hadn't worked her body into this shape to be ashamed before filmmakers. She was the dream that troubled their sleep, lying ageless as they grew older and older.

Joan opened her eyes. The men had gathered around the bed with anxious eyes as if visiting a sick friend.

"Thank you, Joan," the director said. "I find myself still lost in your reading. We will be in touch."

Joan put her clothes on, shook hands with everyone, and left a manila envelope with her résumé and head shot. She rode down in an elevator with cheap golden walls.

"I certainly hope I get that part," she said.

Chapter Four

Jack Snow, the artifacts dealer Dan had been hired to investigate, first came to Grouse County in the winter, fresh out of the federal prison at Lons Ferry, North Dakota, where he'd served federal months for embezzling money from a credit union. He'd had gambling debts. They were not considered a mitigating factor.

FCI Lons Ferry was a cold stone fortress bound by rules, exercise, seniority, the call-out sheet. Prohibited acts ranged from killing to conference calls to kissing.

Jack didn't mind prison as much as he thought he would. You could wear your hair any way you wanted so long as you didn't carve words or figures into it. The barbershop was closed for maintenance on Mondays.

In prison Jack met a man known as Andy from Omaha, with whom he played chess on Wednesdays and Fridays in the yard or the library. Andy gave up knights for bishops any time and took oppressive command of the diagonals. He was serving a long stretch for buying and selling figurines and pottery stolen from excavations around the world.

"I've found the error in my practice," he said one time.

"What's that?" said Jack.

"You take something, somebody will be looking for it. Whereas, a fake, see, nobody's looking for a fake."

"They don't know there is one."

Andy pinned Jack's rook to his king. "Bam," he said.

Andy's work sounded exotic and lucrative compared with robbing the returns of retirees, and he gave Jack a number to call when Jack got out of Lons Ferry. The man who answered the phone told him to find some out-of-the-way place and rent a warehouse.

Having little money, Jack tried staying with people he knew in Stone City. The first turned him down after a few minutes of unfriendly conversation. He lived in a yellow ranch house on an empty hill west of the city—no grove, no outbuildings—and Jack was not disappointed when it didn't work out.

So then he stayed with the other friend, who had a small and neatly kept brick house on New Hampshire Street in town. That lasted till summer, when they argued over a canoe.

It belonged to the friend and one day Jack took it to a used sporting goods place and sold it.

"I figured you'd want it off your hands," he explained when his friend came home. "It's not like you use it."

"What I do with my canoe is my business."

"It hangs behind the garage. That's what you do with it."

"If I never so much as touch the motherfucker that doesn't give you the right to sell it."

"Okay, okay," said Jack. "I was going to take a commission, but you can have it all, if that's how you're going to be."

Jack's friend counted the bills. "That was a nine-hundred-dollar canoe."

"Not all bleached out it wasn't. Did you even look at it lately?"

"Get out."

Jack took a room by the week in the Continental Hotel on the north end of Stone City. This was an ornate stone property built when the railroad came through and falling to ruin ever since. The people who stayed there seemed like ghosts, with unkempt hair and mismatched clothes.

*   *   *

Jack Snow met Wendy, daughter of the couple who would hire Dan, at a fair in the park, where she had set up a folding table to sell moccasins and billfolds.

"Beautiful hobbycraft," said Jack.

Wendy had thick blond hair, small and nimble hands, and a skeptical expression that invited you to talk her out of it.

"When are you supposed to wear moccasins?" said Jack. "Are they bedroom slippers? Can you wear them on the street? Wouldn't the asphalt wear them down?"

"All shoes are damaged by asphalt," said Wendy. "It may surprise you that moccasins hold up better than most. I myself wear them all the time."

She turned sideways on her folding chair and crossed her legs. Jack knelt in the grass and slipped a moccasin from her foot, revealing toenails painted cobalt blue.

Wendy pressed her bare foot to his chest and gave a little shove, setting him back on his heels.

"You should get some for your girlfriend," she said.

"Don't have one. I'm new in town."

"Oh. I see."

They slept together that night in the Continental Hotel. The atmosphere was eeriest at night but Jack found it entertaining in the company of Wendy. They lay in bed listening to the groan of the elevator moving floor to floor. Coughing and faint voices came from other rooms.

"You got a tiger's eyes," said Jack.

"Tiger sounds," she said.

Wendy lived in a duplex by the water tower, and Jack soon moved in with her. He called her Wendell and said no one understood her the way he did, which may have been true.

He liked to watch her remove makeup with gauze pads, mouth open, eyes serious and dark in the mirror. Their sex was bereft and elemental and reminded Jack for some reason of the ranch house on the empty hill.

Wendy cut and sewed her leather pieces at home under a halogen lamp until one or two in the morning. She wore big glasses that made her especially sexy. Sometimes a sadness came over her, and she did not want to do anything, and Jack would feed her cherry ice cream from a spoon.

One summer evening as Jack Snow sat smoking in a nature preserve north of Stone City a man and his long-legged pointer came strolling along.

The dog bounded into the reeds as the man walked the trail, hands in pockets, eyes on the ground. Every once in a while he would whistle and the dog would leap above the weeds, now close, now far.

The man walked over and sat on the bench beside Jack. He called the dog and she came running and sat panting and looking at the man from the corners of her eyes.

"Are you from Omaha?" said Jack.

"Mmm, could be."

"I hope you're happy with what you're getting."

"Wouldn't be here otherwise. We need more of it."

"What do you do with it?"

"Not your concern."

"Who buys it?"

"Nobody."

"I was told I would learn the trade," said Jack.

"This is the trade."

The man stood and the dog looked up. "How'd you get into the Celtic stuff?"

"I had a girlfriend one time who was big on it," said Jack. "Her name was Sandy."

"Was she a Druid?"

"Something like that."

Jack exaggerated—he lied—calling Sandy Zulma his girlfriend. They had been friends as children in the town of Mayall, Minnesota, where they'd played scenes from books of Irish and Welsh legends that she knew and taught to him.

Sometimes she would be Emer to his Cúchulainn, Hound of Ulster, flirting with the young warrior or dying of grief over his body finally brought to ground.

She liked to portray the tragic Deirdre who killed herself rather than live without the betrayed Sons of Usna. They fought the endless battle of the Hound and his old friend Ferdiad, who lost with grief on both sides. And they played chess, because the kings and warriors often did so in the downtime between battles and other adventures.

As teenagers Jack and Sandy went their separate ways. Sandy wanted to keep playing, or perhaps it was no longer play, and Jack fell in with a drinking crowd and gave up their games. When he saw Sandy on the street or in school he would act as if he hardly knew her. He regretted the unkindness.

Louise took the long route home and stopped to see her mother in Grafton. It was after ten but Mary Montrose stayed up late listening to radio shows about paranormal phenomena and the breakdown of society.

Mary's recliner stood in the center of the house on a thronelike platform with its back to the wall. The platform had been built by her friend Hans Cook. Mary had become nervous about storms in her old age—lightning, tornadoes, tree branches breaking through windows—and thought the elevated chair would help her see what was coming.

"Look what the wind carried in," said Mary. "You coming from the junk store?"

"Yep," said Louise, who had long since given up telling Mary it wasn't a junk store. "Have you eaten?"

"I was just about to put something on."

"You lie. You need to eat, Ma."

Mary went to the dining room table and took a seat, blinking in the light. Louise lit a burner on the stove and poured oil into a skillet, tipping it back and forth. She held a bag of frozen shrimp and vegetables and sawed it open with a butcher knife.

"Here, Louise, there's scissors for that," said Mary. "You look like somebody cleaning a fish."

"I wouldn't clean a fish if my life depended on it."

"I bet you would."

"This is true."

Louise slid the frozen block of food into the pan of hot oil, where it made the reassuring racket of frying.

"What's Dan think?" said Mary.

"About what?"

"You running around so late."

"He's all right with it. Why? Did he say something?"

"They go crazy."

"Who does?"

"Men. Get to a certain age. There was a lady on the radio the other night, her husband left her and moved to Phoenix. Baby of the family no more than seven years old."

"What'd he do in Phoenix?

"What didn't he do is more like it. Bought a boat. Wrecked the boat. Got a nurse pregnant."

"Jesus."

"Married the nurse, divorced the nurse. Opened a restaurant, that went bust. Got hepatitis."

Louise put oven mitts on and carried the skillet to the table. "What do you think?"

"I would give that one more minute."

Louise went back to the stove and pushed the seared food around with a wooden spatula. "You shouldn't listen to that morbid junk."

"It *is* morbid."

"Supper is served," said Louise, setting plates on the table.

After they ate, Louise did the dishes and cleaned up the kitchen, and they moved their little party to the living room. Louise made a Twister for herself and tea with brandy for Mary, and they sat looking out the picture window.

Every now and then a car would go around the corner, headlights glancing off the leaves of Mary's trees before pivoting toward the deserted downtown.

They didn't say much. Mary seemed to have talked herself out with the tale of the man who went to pieces in Phoenix. Louise sat on the davenport, one level below her stately mother, her mind floating with the ice in her drink. Around eleven-thirty, she closed the curtains and kissed her mother goodnight.

Mary took her hand. "I won't be here forever, Louise."

"Yes, you will," said Louise. "Your signs are all good. The doctor said. Why? Is something wrong?"

"Not at all. I just want you to know that when I do go? I'll be ready. And that will be why."

"I won't be ready."

"I know. But I wanted to tell you. So you won't have to feel bad."

One afternoon in August Lyris Darling and her boss Don Gary rode out to Rose Hill south of Boris to look at a gravestone with a typographical error. Chrysanthemum bushes were taking over the burial ground, flinging stems and flowers over the long grass. Lyris liked cemeteries wild and abandoned.

They found the monument, on which the inscription was every bit as defective as had been reported by the family. The deceased was named Cynthia and the engravers had transposed the second and third letters of her name.

"This is sad," said Don Gary.

"You want me to call Taber Brothers?" said Lyris.

Don Gary took his glasses off and cleaned them with a handkerchief. "Did we have it right?"

Lyris took their copy of the order from her purse and handed it to him.

"You get Tabers on the phone and you tell them Don Gary is pissed off," he said.

"Okay."

He ran his fingers along the top of the stone. "Actually, don't," he said. "All I need is those fuckers mad at me."

"I'll just say they owe us a new stone."

"Good idea."

They went back to Don Gary's Suburban and drove the perimeter of the cemetery. Don pointed out a memorial with a row of beer cans set carefully before it and observed that tributes evolve with the times and the industry must stay relevant.

As he spoke Lyris saw a black pickup rolling in, tiger-striped with dust. She slouched in her seat.

"It's my grandmother. Keep going."

"I wouldn't think of it," said Don Gary, always eager to meet someone who might someday die.

He stopped and called out the window, and Lyris's grandmother parked her truck beside his and leaned her heavy arm on the door.

"What do you want?" she said.

"I'm Don Gary of Gary Memorials in Stone City. Got somebody here I think you know. Look over here. It's Lyris."

He leaned back, glancing from grandmother to granddaughter, beaming.

"You let her go now," said Colette. She pushed the door of the truck open and it banged the side of the Suburban.

"No, no, no," said Don Gary, his friendly, professional voice gone thin with alarm. "You misunderstand me."

Colette stepped down from the truck with a crowbar in her hand. Lyris skirted the front of the Suburban and took the bar from her grandmother and led her down the space between the vehicles.

"Sorry, Grandma," she said. "That's my boss. He's not kidnapping me. He just can't shut up sometimes."

Colette looked at Don Gary, who was rubbing the side panel of the Suburban with a handkerchief.

"What are you doing in the graveyard?" said Colette.

"One of the headstones is messed up," said Lyris.

"You tell that man not to yell at people he don't know."

"Well, I did tell him that."

"Maybe that's how they do it in Stone City but down here it's bad business."

She unlatched the tailgate of the pickup and let it fall. A red wagon lay wheels up among flats of flowers on the truck bed. Lyris picked up the wagon, set it on the ground, and put the flowers in it.

"Thank you, sweetness. I bet you're missing Micah with him gone."

"Yeah. We didn't see that much of each other after Albert and I started going out. He was jealous, I think."

Colette took the handle of the wagon from the grass. "Did you see any birds this morning?"

"Not that I remember."

"I didn't either." She looked at the trees and the sky. "I'm trying to figure out why."

The old lady trundled among the headstones, pulling the wagon. She had three husbands buried here. She had never spoken well of them and said flowers were a small price to keep them where they belonged.

Don Gary and Lyris drove north to the city. They went several miles before saying anything. Then Don checked his mirrors, cleared his throat, and said, "I imagine nobody pushes her around too much."

"Not too much, Don," said Lyris, watching the roadside for birds.

A faded sign by the desk of the Continental Hotel said that shoes left by eight o'clock in the evening would be shined by eight o'clock the following morning.

Dan Norman showed the manager a photograph of Jack Snow and asked if he recognized him.

"Vaguely," said the manager. He was an old man wearing a starched white shirt, vest, and bow tie. "What'd he do?"

"Maybe nothing," said Dan. "Did he talk to you about his business? Meet with anyone? Did he carry cash beyond the usual?"

"I wouldn't say so."

"Do you remember him at all?"

"You know, I don't."

Dan looked around the lobby. The shades were open but the light did not come in. Four people lay about on frayed furniture. Two watched a game show on television, one sat with folded hands by the window, and the fourth lay with her feet on the back of a couch looking at a big book of railroad pictures.

"Good morning," said the manager over a public-address system the existence of which seemed to surprise everyone. "This is Leon speaking to you once again. If anyone should happen to recall a guest named Jack Snow, please advise the desk."

The woman lying on the davenport closed the book of locomotives and got up. In slate-blue coveralls and black clogs, a red scarf over her hair, she crossed the lobby in long strides.

"I know Jack Snow," she said. "Is he here?"

"In Stone City, I believe he is."

"I think he might have something I want."

"Like what?"

She told Dan about the rock she was after and its possible origins, this time adding that it might be a piece of the stone split by Cúchulainn at Baile's Strand after he killed his son by accident.

"Are you part of his business?" said Dan.

"What business?"

"Celtic artifacts."

"He stole the idea from me."

"What is the idea?"

"Putting the world back together."

Dan understood that the young woman was not in her right mind and gave her his business card, which he found to be a good way to end a conversation.

"You run across Jack Snow, you give me a call," he said.

She read the card and then tucked it into the red scarf above her ear.

"I will, Daniel," she said.

She went back to the davenport and began looking at the picture book again.

"I wouldn't take her too serious," said the manager quietly. "She's not current on her accounts. But I let them go sometimes. They've got to be somewhere. Aren't you the sheriff?"

"One time I was. Do you really shine shoes?"

"Ah, there's no real call for it anymore. Can't shine a tennis shoe."

Sandra laid the railroad book on the rug and climbed the stairs of the Continental Hotel to her room on the fourth floor. She reclined on the bed, head on the pillow, feet against the end rails.

"I am an immortal," she said to the ceiling, as if reassuring herself. "We came to the island of Eire in clouds that blocked the sun three days. From Falias we brought the stone that sings for the true king. The Milesians drove us underground. I washed red clothes in the ford, trying to warn Cúchulainn. But he was too proud to go back."

Then she turned on her side and folded her legs to fit the bed. Sleep was her only happiness. She was sleeping too much. It could not be helped. She would need her strength for what was coming.

Tiny Darling rattled an aluminum pan of scraps and set it in the sun for the goat.

"Who's hungry?" he said.

The goat rocked on silver haunches, building momentum to climb onto the porch.

The phone rang and Tiny went inside. It might have been a job and might have been Micah, but it was only a recording.

"The FBI has learned that houses in your zip code are burglarized once every five seconds," said a woman. "We are in your area now."

"Hell, come on by," said Tiny. "We'll throw some steaks on."

He hung up the phone and went back out to the porch and watched the goat eat.

"I'm told we might be in for some burglaries," Tiny said.

Chapter Five

JOAN HAD to find a school for Micah in the fall. She made packets with an eight-by-ten glossy, transcripts, and an essay he'd written. This is how the essay started:

When I was small I survived a tornado that blew the van in which I was a passenger through a silo. The wind was so loud that all the world and its things seemed to be made of sound waves. Tools floated about like you might pick one from the air as an astronaut would in zero gravity. The tornado taught me that you can get in and out of trouble in unexpected ways. I used to have a goat who would knock things over and pin them with her forelegs as if to say, "Now it is mine." My favorite subject is world history. I think it was a bad deal when the citizen farmers were forced to move to Rome where they had nothing to do in the second century.

Joan thought the essay was thoughtful and creative and she appreciated mention of the tornado which they'd gone through together.

She mailed applications to the Weaving School, Adamantine Prep, Mary Ellen Pleasant Country Day, Brentwood Polyphonic, and Our Lady of Good Counsel on the Hill. None of the schools had an opening for Micah. Our Lady of Good Counsel on the Hill put him on a waiting list.

"That sounds promising," said Joan.

They drove up to the school for an interview. The road climbed the foothills and Joan pointed out a section of roadway that had fallen down a ravine across the valley.

One sunny day of so many Micah took a bus west on Sunset Boulevard to see Thea. Palm trees listed south, leaves fluttering in the wind. The Chateau Marmont rose above trees. He knew it was important but not why.

Billboards lined the boulevard—a bottle of tequila lit up like an altar, a watch too complicated to be useful, a man and two women coated in oil and shirtless in lowrider jeans.

Then the bus went down the hill into Beverly Hills, where businesses and billboards gave way to hardwood groves and hedges and walls and pillars.

Thea's place had a mechanical gate with a warning depicting a stick figure pinned between gate and post, limbs splayed in alarm.

Micah walked up the broad and curving driveway, making way for a plumber's truck that was leaving and got Micah thinking of Tiny. His world and this world seemed to occupy different dimensions. Micah was a traveler who had gone between them.

The house was enormous and ornamental as if a government should be in it and Thea met him out front by a fountain with a statue of a headless woman holding an open book.

"So, this is my crib," said Thea.

"How many people live here?"

"Just us four. My dad built it so his family would have a place to gather. But my aunts and uncles built their houses with the same idea. They're in Ojai and La Jolla and north of San Francisco. So now they can't agree where the family should gather."

They walked around to the back gardens, where hedges radiated from a great tree with smooth gray bark and hundreds of branches thick with purple leaves. Hidden in the leaves was a treehouse with glass windows and cedar shakes.

"God damn," said Micah.

They climbed a ladder to the treehouse. It was messy inside. Clothes and books and food wrappers lay wherever Thea had dropped them. Micah began picking things up and organizing them and Thea joined him.

"I spend a lot of time here," she said. "I don't sleep well in the house. The vertical space is oppressive."

The treehouse had a futon, a bumper pool table, a refrigerator, a desk, and a chair. They played pool. Thea leaned over the table, biting her lower lip with her little front teeth. She won the game in no time. Bumper pool was harder than Micah thought.

"Well, I get so much practice," she said. "You'll get better the more you play."

"Then you'll invite me back."

"Of course. As now we are friends."

After the game they sat on the futon and Thea took a dark green tin in her lap, opened it, and rolled a joint. She lit up and inhaled, waving her hand beside her throat.

"What do you think of Charlotte?" she said.

"Is she in those Boston shoe ads?"

"Yeah. Hold it in."

Micah held his breath. "I like the one when they're on a boat," he said in a deep voice.

"I want you to think about something. Charlotte's going around with people who aren't good for her. They drink all the time, and the only reason they follow her is . . . well, you know how she looks."

"Yeah, beautiful," said Micah. "You both are."

Her ears turned red, just like that. "I'm not Charlotte."

"You're very pretty, in my opinion."

She looked at him sadly, as if trying to arrange the thousand and one things he didn't know into a manageable list.

"Have you ever asked anybody out?"

"Sure," said Micah. "Well, not really."

"I want you to ask Charlotte out."

"Isn't she kind of old for me?"

"How old are you?"

"Fourteen."

"Hmmm." Thea was quiet, and Micah thought she might forget the whole idea.

"That is young," she said. "But I saw how she looked at you, Micah. She really cared about you, making sure your high was okay. That was the old Charlotte."

"Where would I ask her out to?"

"It's not a big thing. Just say you'll get some coffee."

Micah agreed and Thea hugged him. He climbed down from the treehouse, walked out the way they had come, opened the gate, and waited half an hour for a bus.

The lights were coming on over Sunset and people sat talking in restaurants that spilled onto the sidewalks. Hollywood pigeons strolled the globe of the Cinerama Dome.

Eamon was typing on a laptop and watching *History's Mysteries* in the family room when Micah got home. The TV showed an aerial view of a metal warehouse among trees.

"Soon sounds of hammering and sawing begin to emanate from their headquarters," said the narrator.

"What is this?" said Micah.

"I don't know. World War II something or other."

Eamon muted the television. The scene cut to two men sitting at a table covered with blueprints. They seemed elated over whatever they were building.

"Did you ever go out with Charlotte?" said Micah.

"Sophomore year."

"What happened?"

"We stopped."

"How come?"

"We just did. Why?"

Micah sat down and retied the laces of his sneakers. "I was think-ing of asking her to have coffee."

"Everybody falls in love with Charlotte. It's like a law of nature. Gravity, then Charlotte."

"It's not love. It's coffee. Thea said I should."

"You're a big coffee drinker, huh?"

"No. I hate it."

"Have latte. But now, Thea told you. This is interesting. Where did you see Thea?"

"At her treehouse."

"Really." Eamon gave Micah a little push. "You're just the latest thing, aren't you?"

Early every morning Joan ran in the park. She did not wear ear-phones but heard music in her head, *Ode to Joy* or *Alegria* or *The Munsters Theme*. One day at the soccer field she saw a young woman sleeping on the grass. Coming closer, she realized that it was Char-lotte Mann.

Charlotte wore a short black dress, one red shoe, and a black leather jacket with rawhide fringe and brass studs. She was asleep on an orange blanket in the grass. Joan covered her legs and touched her shoulder.

Charlotte sat up and looked around and scratched the back of her head with both hands. Unbraided, her hair fell in waves to her shoulders.

"Well, this is embarrassing," she said.

She got up, took the blanket by two corners, and gave it a shake. Cigarettes and a lighter shot from the blanket. She walked toward them, crooked on one shoe.

"What happened?" said Joan.

Charlotte flopped down, took the shoe off, lit a cigarette, and blew a smoke ring. "What time is it?"

"Twenty after seven."

"What day is it?"

"Tuesday."

"Do you see my phone?"

Joan looked around. "How did you get here?"

"I don't remember. We were at a house and then we were at a club. Then maybe a house again. Or that might have been the first house. People kept stepping on my ankles. Maybe I'll stay here till someone comes."

"No one is coming. It's morning."

"They might be driving ever so slowly."

"Charlotte. Honey. Wake up. You can't be doing this to yourself."

They walked across the soccer field. Wearing the blanket like a shawl, Charlotte dropped the mateless shoe into a trash can.

"I'm sorry you found me this way."

"You don't have to worry about your place with me," said Joan. "I know you. I know what my boys think of you. You have a good heart."

"No I don't. My heart is a mess."

Micah and Charlotte did not go for coffee. Instead she picked him up in a small yellow Datsun pickup and they drove up to Mount Wilson on Angeles Crest Highway. Charlotte wore khaki shorts, green sneakers, and a pink tank top with a border of shiny green stones against her copper skin.

The mountain road climbed, steep with switchbacks. Rocks had fallen in the roadway, and Charlotte cranked the wheel, steering carefully around them. The sky was deep blue, with lavender clouds around faraway peaks.

A famous observatory stood on top of the mountain, white domes rising from forests with pinecones big as footballs. Charlotte knew all about the place. George Hale had worked here, and Edwin Hubble. Observations of the sun gave way to observations of all space. Einstein came up to talk things over. The universe expanded.

Micah and Charlotte looked at Hubble's chair in the gloomy vault of the Hooker Telescope while listening to a recording by someone named Hugh Downs. The chair appeared to have been borrowed from the Hubbles' dining room table.

"Imagine being Hubble," said Charlotte.

"I can't. He's too smart."

"It's late, it's cold. You write down this number, you turn some dial, you write down another number."

"Something doesn't add up."

"The things you are learning are going to turn this world upside down."

They were quiet then. Breathing quickly, Charlotte ran her hands beneath her hair and lifted it back over her shoulders. They walked down with the voice of Hugh Downs fading in the stairwell.

They ate at the Cosmic Cafe in a wooded pavilion between the observatory and the parking lot. Charlotte drove past a cluster of communications towers and a little way down the mountain before stopping at a turnout.

A dusty trail took them along the mountain wall, where they sat cross-legged on a flat rock projecting over nothing. Someone had run a power line out here on scarred poles, but the line stopped and there was one last pole in the sand with nothing attached to it.

"Look at that," said Micah.

Charlotte stared at the column of sky, drawing her knees up and wrapping her arms around them. "Would you mind if I bit you on the arm?" she said.

"Is this a hypothetical question?"

"I wouldn't break the skin."

"Why?"

"I don't know. Sometimes I just get nervous and have to bite something. Do you know what I mean?"

"Do it to yourself how you would do it."

She raised her forearm to her mouth and bit. Her eyes opened wide. Then she presented her arm and they examined it together.

Slowly the pale white of teeth marks turned the lion-mane color of her skin.

"Are you afraid it will hurt?" she said.

"Does it?"

She shrugged. "Some?"

Micah rolled the sleeve of his work shirt above the elbow and brushed off his arm.

"Do you want to?" she said.

"Can't be that bad."

"Good man! I'm so excited." She gathered her hair in an elastic band, settled beside him, and took his arm in both hands, drawing the two of them shoulder to shoulder.

"Now you say when to stop," she said.

"Okay."

She bent her head and closed her eyes. At first Micah felt only the warmth of her mouth and the softness of her lips.

Her teeth closed, gathering a cord of flesh. It didn't hurt much at first, and then he felt the pressure inside his arm. He saw that it would be easy to play this game till blood was drawn.

Charlotte opened her mouth when she realized he would not call it off. Her teeth had left an oval of perfect dashes, inside of which the hair on his arm was swirled and wet. His arm cooled as it dried.

He looked at her and saw that she had tears in her eyes and realized that he did too. Maybe the bite had hurt more than he thought and maybe it was something else. They leaned their faces one toward the other without thinking and kissed for a long time.

This was Micah's first kiss, and he knew he would remember it all his life. When it was over they sat with their hands on the hot flat rock and legs stretched before them.

Chapter Six

SOMETIMES ALBERT Robeshaw wrote little profiles for the Stone City newspaper. He would drive around waiting for someone to catch his eye: an ice skater, a hobo, a bat biologist —someone doing something different that could be told in four hundred words.

Late one afternoon he happened on Sandra Zulma practicing sword moves with a yardstick by the war memorial. She paused in her routine as Albert introduced himself.

"I'll tell you my story," she said, "but first you have to buy me a drink."

Albert agreed, thinking this would make a good beginning. They crossed the street and walked down to a tavern called Bruiser's, Sandra tapping the yardstick on the sidewalk like a blind woman.

Albert bought beers, took them to the booth, and opened his notebook to an empty page. Sandra talked as Albert took notes. After a while he stopped taking notes.

According to Sandra, she had come to the Midwest in a tunnel that ran beneath the ocean. She didn't know how long this took. Months, probably, or a year. The tunnel was smooth and well lighted at first but eventually became dark and cold and narrow. She starved and stumbled; the rocks cut her hands and feet. Finally she collapsed, falling into a deep sleep.

When she woke her hair had grown long and matted, her clothes turned to rags. She saw a light that had not been there before. Either she'd walked without knowing or someone had moved her. She crawled to the end of the tunnel, coming out on a ledge above a river.

A troop of Boy Scouts waded across and handed up a canteen of water and she drank it all down and stood howling above the Scouts while flocks of birds flew from the ravine.

"I wonder if you shouldn't talk to someone about your stories," said Albert.

"I'm talking to you."

"Someone more like a doctor."

Sandra set the yardstick on edge, and there it stood. "Doctors don't know anything. What is your blood pressure? Do you have thoughts of hurting yourself or others? That's what they know. Don't be afraid. You will never find a truer friend than me. We can sleep together in the Continental Hotel."

Albert drew an exclamation point on his reporter's notebook. "I'm not sure this is working out," he said.

At that moment the owner of the bar came up from the basement with a bottle of tequila. When he saw Sandra he hurried across the barroom.

"What did I say about that stick?" he said.

"Remind me," said Sandra.

"You're not to come in here with that."

Sandra smiled. "Well, too bad, because I already have, and this is a public place."

The True Value yardstick of wheat-colored wood and black fractions lay across the table with Sandra's hand hovering.

"If you can take it from me," she said, "I will scrub tables in this bar for one year without pay."

"I wouldn't even *want* that."

The bar owner and Albert reached for the yardstick, which jumped to Sandra's hand. She slashed the stick through the air, hitting the man in the throat. He fell back, knocked over a chair, dropped the bottle he was carrying, and held his neck with his hands.

Albert and Sandra stepped from the booth, holding opposite ends of the yardstick and circling each other as in some ritual. A smile came over Sandra's face, and a reddish light shone around her white hair. She yanked on the yardstick, Albert lurched forward, and she struck his face with the heel of her hand, at which point he let go. She backed to the door of Bruiser's as Albert and the bar patrons gathered warily around her.

"First one to move is the last one to get up," she said.

They considered the sequence implied by the threat. With one hand behind her back, Sandra found the doorknob and slipped out of the bar. They saw her walking past the window.

"Is she a friend of yours?" said the barman.

"I just met her," said Albert.

"That crazy fuck does not come in here again."

Don Gary's tombstone dealership closed for the day, and Lyris sat on the steps, waiting for Albert and looking at the moon above the city. Don Gary locked the door and walked past her in his brown saddle shoes.

"Goodnight, Miss Darling," he said.

"Goodnight, Don."

Lyris liked it at night when she was alone and Albert on his way. She felt free and original with him, their old lives like train cars uncoupled and falling away.

When he drove up she got in the car and kissed him. He had a bruise under his eye and driving home told her of his attempt to interview Sandra Zulma.

Back at the apartment Lyris led Albert by the hand to the bathroom, where they stood looking at the welt on his cheekbone in the medicine cabinet mirror.

Albert said it was nothing but Lyris insisted on treating it. She washed and dried her hands and took a small green bottle from the medicine chest.

Albert sat on the toilet lid looking up at the light fixture as she painted antiseptic beneath his eye with a stiff black brush built into the cap of the bottle.

"Now it looks really terrible," she said.

Then, for no reason other than play, she painted a stripe under the other eye.

"Now you're a football player."

"She never hit me there."

"Oh, I like this look."

They went into the bedroom and closed the door. The room was dark except for the light from the windows.

He undressed her, rolled her black tights down. Lyris breathed slowly, fingers trembling at her sides. Being with Albert was more than she'd ever expected. They liked making love in the early hours of the night, when time lay like emptiness before them. They liked being close to coming. The blue light from the street made a halo around the bed.

Two hours went by. The softest kiss of the night and they rested, flat on their backs beneath a sheet. Lyris traced with her fingers the marks she had painted on his face. Albert slept. She crossed his body with her leg and lay her head on his shoulder. This was the best, the most bearable loneliness.

Lyris's bad dream was of places—rooms in the orphanage, in foster homes, in Grouse County. Other rooms she did not know yet, maybe would never know.

She saw them from above. Apparently she was on some kind of catwalk. The rooms went by one by one as in a slideshow, dimly lit and empty of people, with tables and chairs, beds and cupboards. Maybe the future had come, when everything alive would be swept away.

All Lyris had to do was decide which room should be hers and claim it. But it was a long way down. The fall could hurt her. It seemed more logical that she should just appear in the room but that didn't seem to be happening. Meanwhile her chance to be anywhere at all was slipping away, leaving her stranded in this cold nowhere, and she called for help.

"What is it?" said Albert. In confusion he'd gone to the windows.

She slid on her back across the mattress and took him by the arm, pulling him to the bed.

"Help me wake up," she said.

Ned Kuhlers was the most influential lawyer in Grouse County. Once Dan's adversary, he was now his biggest client. He had an office above the park with a tropical fish tank running the length of the reception area.

Ned's secretary pushed a button on the intercom. "Dan Norman's here."

"Get that bastard in here."

Dan entered Ned's office and sank into a green leather chair with brass grommets running along the seams.

"What's different?" said Ned.

"The clock is slow, the fern is dying, and there's a stain on the paneling that appears to be oil of some kind," said Dan. "Likely you were eating at your desk and shook up a bottle of salad dressing and the top wasn't on right."

Ned laughed. He'd boxed flyweight in the merchant marines and would sometimes move his hands fast to make people flinch.

"Correct on some counts," he said. "Anyway. You will like this. My client had a car accident. He pulled out on 33 and plowed into some other guy. Now, we're not contesting fault. We had the stop. So be it. But it turns out the other driver is a bowler. Do you bowl?"

"Not often."

"I know. The pins go up, they come down, so what. But this guy loves bowling so much that it gives him pain and suffering not to."

"Since the accident."

"They say he'll never bowl again."

"Too bad."

"Yes, but for the simple fact that he is bowling," said Ned. "Just doing it where he won't be seen. Moved from the Rose Bowl in Morrisville to Rust River Lanes."

"In Romyla."

"Tuesdays at nine o'clock."

"Probably trying to get his form back."

"You're either bowling or you're not bowling."

"You want pictures," said Dan.

"I want video."

"What's he look like?"

Ned tossed a manila envelope across the desk and Dan caught it.

Dan figured he could use a partner, as one lone-wolf bowler might notice another. He asked his assistant Donna, who was always up for anything undercover. She'd been Woman A in Lord Norman's exposure of sexist hiring patterns at Airstream Creamery in Morrisville.

Dan told her to dress naturally, but when he arrived at her house she came out wearing an orange mohair half-sleeved sweater, a strapless white dress with black polka dots and flared skirt, shimmery green anklets and heels. She got in the car, gathered the papery folds of the dress, and shut the door.

"Let's do some bowling," she said.

"Nice outfit, but the idea is not to draw attention," said Dan.

"Say you were doing something secret," she said. "Wouldn't the person trying not to draw attention be exactly the one you'd worry about?"

"That almost makes sense," said Dan.

Romyla served as a bedroom town for both Morrisville and Stone City, though the Romylans did not like the term, as it made them seem less than the whole show. Rust River Lanes had eight alleys on Main Street in a building that had once been a bank. A big pin stood on the roof of the building, but it was not lighted, so at night it looked like an apparition.

Dan and Donna got shoes from the counter and glasses of beer and took a lane two up from the man who had been broadsided on Route 33. A sign on the wall set out the rules.

NO SMOKING

NO LOFTING

NO CURSING

NO FIREWORKS

NO GESTURES

Dan placed a small and cunning video recorder on the scorer's table. The works were concealed in a Fanta pop can with a button on top that turned the camera on and off. Lynn Lord had made it himself. They called it the Fanta cam and it took HD video and stills.

Everyone's hands are low at some point in their bowling delivery, but Donna kept her hands low throughout. She wove her way to the line as if herding small animals in a party dress.

The ball rolled slowly, and the pins fell wearily in on themselves, leaving splits. Dan's release point was inconsistent, and he'd usually end up with a blister on his thumb. Together they seemed bad enough to be innocent bowlers.

The target of their investigation bowled like a man on the tour. He whipped his arm around and finished with gloved hand held high and pins flying like pheasants from grass.

When it got to be ten-thirty and they had bowled long enough to seem credible, Dan drove Donna home and parked beside the tall and narrow house in Mixerton where she rented the top floor.

"We make a good team, teammate," she said.

"Ned will be happy."

"Who cares."

"He's the client."

"You knew when you asked me. I knew. I didn't say anything."

"Knew what?"

"You wanted my company. People need each other's company. That's all right." She smoothed her dress. "I made myself nice. Life goes on a little while and then it's over."

"Donna, I didn't mean to give you the idea that, um, well, that this was—"

"And I suppose all my ideas come from you."

"I didn't say that."

"You don't know what you're saying."

Dan leaned down to give her a friendly kiss or maybe she was right and he didn't know what he intended. Anyway it's not what happened.

They made out in the car, her dress rustling like fire. He pressed her hair back and kissed her lips. He knew he'd feel terrible when the kiss was over, but it seemed natural as could be in the moment.

A car drove down the quiet road, the light passing over them. Dan got out of the car and went around to open her door. Millers swarmed around a streetlamp.

"Do you want to come up?" said Donna.

"Truth is I do, Donna. But what I ought to do is go home."

"Okay, Dan. But you know what?"

"What?"

"Some things are not serious."

Louise kept thinking of Lyris and Albert's apartment. At an estate auction in Chesley she outbid competitors for a fine oak table and a copper pan rack and had them delivered to the third floor of the Kleeborg Building.

That night after closing she took her toolbox and went upstairs. The table and rack waited in the hallway. Albert answered the door in his stocking feet.

"Hi," he said. "I was just watching a special about the yeti."

"How's he doing?"

"He might be a bear."

"That's no fun."

"Is that Louise?" called Lyris from inside.

"Yeah," said Albert.

"Tell her she's got to stop."

"You can't keep giving us stuff," said Albert.

"Don't you like them?"

"The table I love. The other thing I don't know what it is."

"I'll show you."

The kitchen had an island and Louise and Lyris climbed onto it to install the pan rack, which would hang suspended from chains. Lyris held the hardware while Louise drilled holes in the ceiling as thin columns of powdered plaster drifted down.

"I've always wanted one of these," said Louise. "I see them in magazines and they make me think the people must have lots of friends."

It was hot near the ceiling and Lyris wiped sweat from her cheek with the back of her hand. Louise wondered what reason on earth kept her from leaving this poor young couple be.

Albert leaned against the counter and watched them working. "I think I'll go out to a bar or something," he said.

The women looked down on him. "I could kick you from here," said Lyris.

"But would you?"

"No."

When the rack was installed and level Albert helped them down from the island and they hung pots and pans and a big spoon and stood watching them turn slowly in the air.

"I can't believe this is really our kitchen," said Lyris.

Albert and Louise carried the table in from the hallway, and Lyris brought the leaves that went with it. The table was well made and heavy, with stout spindle legs rarely found, and they would rest and lean on it now and then.

They put the table in the dining room, pulled the ends apart, laid the leaves on the rails, aligning pegs and holes, and pushed the table snugly back together.

"I love putting leaves in tables," said Albert. "It's the only thing I used to like about holidays at home."

He rounded up chairs and Lyris got a bottle of wine and poured three drinks and they sat at the table and raised their glasses.

"To Louise," said Lyris.

"This is a big table," said Albert. "We will need to have many children."

"I don't know why you're being so nice to us," said Lyris.

"No special reason," said Louise. "That's what mothers do, isn't it?"

She closed her eyes and laughed softly.

"Jesus," she said. "Where did that come from. I'm sorry. What friends do."

Albert drank his wine. The yeti show played in the living room, a storm howling in the mountains.

"It's all right," said Lyris. "I know what you mean."

Louise covered her embarrassed smile with her hand and shook her head. "I think I will be going."

She drove home in the Scout II, shifting gears harshly. She listened to the radio for a while, shut it off, and punched the dashboard.

What she said came out so easily. In that moment, when they were relaxed and together, she must have believed it.

At the farm, yellow leaves scratched and spun across the yard. The lights were on in the house, but she would not go in yet. She sat in the truck with her hands on her face, looking out over the tops of her fingers.

She was a mother, though who would remember? Her daughter died at birth sixteen years ago. Louise almost died too. If she had, she wondered, would she and the girl be together? In any way that they were aware of, she meant.

Sometimes she thought of Iris, imagined the life she would have had. Watching television, putting on Louise's makeup, riding in cars with reckless boys. Or playing soccer, running and kicking, hair flying in the wind.

*   *   *

Dan Norman had learned of Jack Snow's prison term, which would satisfy his clients' desire to discredit him in their daughter's eyes. He still wondered what Jack and Wendy were doing in the warehouse.

He staked it out, watching with binoculars from the trainyard. They worked bankers' hours, arriving in the red Mustang. Parcel trucks came and went. There was one visitor, a lady who went inside and left half an hour later.

Dan ran her license plates and found that she was a professor named Mildred at the community college in Stone City. He found her one day in her office, a small room musty with books at the end of a hallway in the Culture, Media and Sport Annex.

She was a tall woman, in her sixties, Dan guessed, with long brown hair and a gray felt hat with a black ribbon on the side.

"Mr. Snow put up a notice on a bulletin board looking for someone to appraise Celtic relics," she said. "I was curious. And the truth is, I could use the money. Part-time college professors are not highly paid in this area."

"You went, you talked to him," said Dan.

"They're not real," she said. "He's tried to make them look old, but I don't know who they would fool. They're not, they don't, no."

"What does he do to them?"

"Tarnishing solutions, crude abrasives. I believe he wraps some of the larger items in blankets and hits them with a two-by-four."

"So you say, Whoa, this stuff is no good."

"Something like that. And he suggested that I could estimate what they'd be worth if they were real, and I said I didn't think that would be a very wise use of my time."

"Good call," said Dan.

"I was disappointed."

"Where are these things from, Ireland?"

"Being copies, I suppose they could be from anywhere. The designs are most likely based on excavations in Europe, Britain, and Ireland. The Celts, you know, were not a single culture, and would not have referred to themselves as 'Celts.' They were a lot of different people who spoke a similar language and lived all across central Europe at one time, from Ireland to the Balkans and as far east as Asia Minor."

Mildred beamed, giving knowledge.

"I had no idea," said Dan.

"Say, 200 B.C.E.," she said. "The Greeks called them *Keltoi*. But then came the Romans and the Germans, and the Celtic speakers of Europe were mostly defeated. I mean, it didn't happen all at once. Over several centuries. The reason we think of Ireland is that Ireland evaded Romanization. So it was there that many of the stories were written."

Dan drove out to the warehouse that night, pried open a window in back, and climbed in. He did not mind breaking laws now that he was not in charge of keeping them. The transgression amounted to nothing against making out with Donna behind Louise's back.

He shined a flashlight down the long and narrow space. Metal shapes glinted on tables. The air smelled of sulfur.

One table held steel swords and scabbards, some new, some in degrees of decomposition. They were simple—broad tapered blades, with crossguards and without. Dan picked one up, tossed it hand to hand. The grip had spiral ridges, making it easy to hold. Dan ran a finger down the blade, drawing a bead of blood that he wiped on his sleeve.

And so he went through the warehouse, examining helmets, tiaras, crowns, stone and bronze figurines of people and animals with shapes softened as if by fire, a horse with a human face, countless pins and rings and C-shaped neck pieces, oval shields with carvings and eroded edges.

Snooping in the dark, he felt the magic going on here. It was a common magic, as in a gun shop or camera store where people gather around things that have been made and become excited. And why? he wondered. What would account for that. Maybe an ingrained love of tools, from caveman days. Things are not what they seem.

The workbenches were laid out with rasps and saws and ball-peen hammers and sealed plastic containers of many sizes. He opened one and clapped it shut because of the smell. In a clawfoot bathtub, a sword lay submerged in dark greenish liquid. Dan kicked the tub with his boot and a tremor ran the length of the sword.

"What a strange job," he said.

Having spoken, Dan felt the presence of someone watching or listening. This did not concern him. He would have the upper hand.

There was a door in a corner of the warehouse, and Dan opened it and stepped into a small room with windows. There was an erasable board on the wall with the optimistic title "Shipping and Receiving."

In a desk he found a cash box and a revolver. He removed the bullets from the gun and put them in his pocket and left, taking nothing else from the warehouse.

CHAPTER SEVEN

Micah entered Deep Rock Academy in the fall—Eamon went there, and the school was obliged to admit his stepbrother. Deep Rock stands on a hill north of Los Angeles, in Sun Terrace, west of Shadowland, built in the style of a Spanish castle. Round towers anchor the corners, and it was a tower that would get Micah in trouble.

All the students at Deep Rock must do something to care for the school. Micah disinfected the drinking fountains, a humble task but one that allowed him to wander the hallways and the upper floors, where the seniors lounged at their lockers, more handsome and worldly than the teachers.

Micah carried a bucket of cleaner and a sponge on a stick. One day, trying the door to the northeast tower, he found it unlocked and went up the spiral staircase, running his free hand over the gritty bricks. There could be a drinking fountain up there. It was not impossible.

Micah came out on top of the school, where the California flag flew. The bear on the flag trudged along, head down and mouth open, following a red star. The view was panoramic—cars on the freeway, dusty horse farms, low houses with yards of sand and tufted grass. He felt far from home.

Then the door opened, and the headmaster came up. Many rumors went around about the large and well-dressed Mr. Lyons. He'd been a psychiatrist, an oilman, an admiral in the Navy, a double agent. He knew secrets about the board of directors that would keep him headmaster for life. Joan claimed that he'd once put Eamon in a coffin for writing something on his desk.

The headmaster put on sunglasses and lit a cigar. "Who told you to come up here?"

"No one."

"Go to the edge. Look down."

Micah leaned into a notch in the wall and saw the ground far below, scrub grass and white rocks disappearing in shadow.

"What would happen if you fell?"

"I would die."

"And how would that look?"

"If I was dead?"

"How would it look for the school?"

"Oh. Pretty bad."

Mr. Lyons puffed on the cigar and looked at it as all cigar smokers must for some reason. "People would say, 'See there? They can't even keep students from falling off the school.'"

"I wasn't planning on falling."

"No one plans to fall till they do. Do you know what this tower is for?"

"Looks?"

"It's for me to smoke. Unless you want a cigar I don't see any reason for you to be here."

"Cigars make me sick."

"That passes. What's your name?"

"Micah Darling."

"You just got your first detention, Micah Darling. Are you the one with the goat?"

Micah nodded.

"That means nothing to me."

"I'll leave now."

"What's your sport?"

"I don't have one."

"Volleyball is your sport. Sign up now."

"Yes, sir."

"And you have detention for the next three days. In this school I am king. Don't prize yourself above others. Stay out of the towers."

When Joan learned of Micah's detention, she called a family meeting. Micah tried to talk her out of it, but once the idea had occurred to her she became fond of it.

And so they all gathered one evening in the library, a dark room with a chandelier that was a replica of a famous one in some opera house. The armchairs were large and leather-bound, and the family took their seats like actors in a play.

"We all need to be aware," said Joan. "It shouldn't be Joan deals with Micah and Rob deals with Eamon. What we face, we face together."

"Micah went into the tower, right?" said Rob.

"There was no sign," said Joan. "The door was not locked."

"Still, it seems reasonable. You can't go everywhere."

"I knew I shouldn't," said Micah.

"I don't trust Mr. Lyons," said Joan. "He seems to have it in for our family. I thought the same thing when he put Eamon in a coffin for writing Charlotte's name on his desk."

Micah sighed. Now this image that meant so much to her would be revealed as imaginary. Perhaps it recalled to her a scene from a vampire movie.

"It wasn't a coffin, Joan," said Eamon. "It was a closet."

Rob picked a bit of lint from his sweater and brushed the cloth with his fingers. "Joan may exaggerate, but I didn't like that closet business either."

"I do not exaggerate," said Joan. "I distinctly remember a coffin."

"Why would there be a coffin at the school?" said Rob.

Micah prayed the family talk would end. By his presence he drew Joan into strange variations on motherly behavior. She'd found herself a good situation and he didn't want to be the one that messed it up.

"It *felt* like a coffin," Eamon said helpfully.

The phone rang. Joan picked it up, went to a corner, talked while idly spinning a globe. Then she came back smiling her beautiful smile.

"I'm going to be in a movie," she said.

They celebrated with brandy, happy for Joan and happier still that the family meeting was done.

The Powder Horn would actually be her second film. She had played a hand-wringing wife in *Shovel Boys*, about boyhood friends who team up later in life to rig a race at Santa Anita. "What do you even *know* about horse racing?" had been her big line.

Detention amounted to sitting in study hall and doing homework with other kids in detention. It was no big thing, except that much of the homework baffled Micah, which was another problem.

Charlotte Mann picked him up on the last night. She wore camo riding pants and a thermal shirt of quilted purple. She hugged him, her legs taut as bowstrings. California girls must hug twenty times a day, Micah thought, their lives teeming with affection.

"I told Joan I'd come get you," she said. "I owe her a favor."

"For what?"

"She helped me one time I was passed out in the park."

They walked to the parking lot and got into her yellow pickup. She put it in reverse, peering up at the school.

"This place is like a prison," she said.

Micah rolled down the window and rested his arm on the door. "They forced me to play volleyball."

"Where did you go before?"

"Boris-Chesley Regional Middle School. We had an English teacher one time, he said, 'Cauliflower is just garbage with a college education.'"

"What did he mean by that?"

"Cabbage with a college education."

"You should take me there sometime."

"They wouldn't believe you."

"That's all right," said Charlotte. "I don't believe myself sometimes. You want to go straight home?"

"Not especially."

So they drove out to Topanga to see her filly, which they didn't get to see last time because they got high and looked at helicopters.

The horse was a Dutch warmblood named Pallas Athena. In her stall Charlotte showed Micah how scratching Pallas at the base of her mane made her lift her head and move her lips strangely, as if talking to herself.

Charlotte tacked the horse with saddle and bridle, easing the bit in with cupped hand. She put on a plastic helmet and mounted up.

Micah had ridden three times, got thrown once. He found horses hard to read. Their thoughts might go back to the beginning of horse time, or they might be afraid of a candy wrapper on the ground. He was wary of anything that big that bit.

Charlotte rode the horse at a walk to the ring. Micah opened the gate and let the shadow of the horse pass by and latched the gate and stood leaning on the fence with his arms over the rail. The sun was down. Lights shone around the ring.

Horse and rider walked and trotted for a while and then picked up a canter. Charlotte pushed Pallas forward with her hips. Mane and braids rose and fell in rhythm. Pallas's hooves drummed on sand and her breath went huff, huff, huff.

Charlotte began to work the horse in figure eights the length of the ring, taking jumps with planters of flowers or small trees on either side. She leaned long over Pallas's neck, the horse rising as if levitated by her hands. They seemed to calculate together the steps before a jump, and when they landed their heads turned as one toward the next gate.

Then two kids came down from the barns, calling Charlotte's name in singsong voices. She brought Pallas down to a walk and spoke to the boys from the saddle as she went along the railing.

The boys turned to look at Micah, and he glanced away at the tall and shaggy trees across the ring. They came over and introduced themselves as Doc and Dalton.

"Are you going to be a doctor?" Micah said.

Doc shook his head. He had a narrow face and luminous green eyes and was a little scary in appearance, like he had handguns at home.

"I used to wear scrubs," he said. "Somebody said I looked like a doctor, so that's how it got started."

"I thought you started it," said Dalton.

"What do *you* know?"

"That you gave yourself a nickname, which is a sad and lonely thing to do. Don't you agree, Micah?"

Pallas Athena was trotting formally, neck arched, nose down, knees high. "I wouldn't be the one to say," said Micah.

Dalton carried a red and white cooler, from which he took bottles of beer and passed them around. He had long hair, a red beret, a wide and placid smile.

"So why are you here?" he said. "Do you have designs on Charlotte?"

"I'm watching."

"How hard it is to wait for one's heart's desire," said Doc.

"Who said that?" said Dalton.

"I think it was Babar."

Dalton collared Micah's head with his arm. "Here's the thing about Charlotte. You might even want to write it down. Everyone wants her, but no one can have her."

"Even when she's drunk," said Doc.

"That's when she's most like an angel."

"A falling angel."

"Just be quiet," said Micah.

"Are you Irish?"

"No."

"You sound it."

When Charlotte had finished her ride she brought Pallas to the gate and the boys swung it open.

"We were talking about you," said Dalton.

"Who cares," she said.

"Trying to get your friend to open up."

"He's like a clam in a clamshell," said Doc.

"No one can talk when you're talking."

"That is kind of true. Listen, we're not going to wait around for the tedious unshackling of the horse. And you're coming, now, right?"

"I don't know."

"Come on," said Doc. "We said you were."

"There is anticipation," said Dalton. "You too, Irish. It's a party."

Charlotte walked the horse around the barn and into an alley between stalls. She dismounted, loosened the girth and ran the stirrups up, exchanged the bridle for a green halter.

"Don't mind them," she said.

"I don't."

"Why'd they call you 'Irish'?"

"My voice, I guess."

"They're just thoughtless boys," said Charlotte. "One time we were at somebody's house, and a dog got into Dalton's backpack and ate some pills. So everyone's going, 'Oh no, this is terrible, should we call the vet?' And Dalton said, 'No, it's fine. They're *for* dogs.'"

From the horse farm Charlotte and Micah went to a party on the roof of a loft building in the Toy District. They rode up in an elevator and, holding hands, made their way down a sandalwood walk lined with path lights and waxy plants.

There were many people, a luminous blue swimming pool, and a bar. The skyscrapers of Los Angeles bent overhead in bands of light. Doc and Dalton dangled their legs from atop a brick shed with silver ducts climbing the walls. Bartenders in white shirts and bow ties poured drinks from silver pitchers.

That Micah should not be here, that he was too young, that he knew no one—all these things did not matter. With Charlotte by his side, the world opened as he'd always dreamed it might.

They got drinks and settled into a sunken space with cushioned benches. The drinks had salt crusted on the rims.

"What are these?" said Micah.

"Margaritas," said Charlotte.

After two drinks Micah could admit to himself that he loved Charlotte. She was not beholden to him but seemed to find something that interested her, God knows what, for he considered himself unaccomplished and lacking in basic skills.

She drank fast, watching the party, the people gathering and drifting apart in the darkness. Facets of the glass magnified her upper lip. She got half a glass ahead of him and they lost track of who was leading, who chasing. At some point she went away and didn't come back for a long time.

Micah thought it would be a good time for a smoke. He didn't smoke, but many people were doing so, and it seemed worth trying.

"Excuse me, I wonder if I could have a cigarette," he said to a woman in a long red shirt that look soft and touchable.

She gave him a cigarette and lent him her lighter. He had trouble with it, so she took it back and lit his cigarette.

"Nice party," he said.

He had decided recently that everything he said sounded artificial, and he would not fight it. He was acting. The woman gave him a dubious smile while putting the lighter away. She wore green velvet shoes of elvish design.

"How old are you?" she said.

"I will be fifteen in November."

"What the hell, we've got fifteen-year-olds here?" she said.

Micah nudged her with his shoulder. "In *November* I'll be fifteen. And how old are you?"

"You're rather bold."

"You asked me."

She looked at him as if half wishing someone would come and take him away, but then, half not. "I did, didn't I. I'm thirty-two."

"That must be a nice age. I think I would like to be thirty-two."

"And why is that?"

"If you want to go somewhere, you just get in the car and go. That in itself is a tremendous advantage. You have your own place. I'm assuming that you do. I don't know that."

"You're at it."

"Well, okay. That's what I'm talking about. And you can put pictures on the wall, and when your friends come over, they'll say, 'Hey, I like what you're doing with this place.'"

Later he was talking to Charlotte again. They were on top of the air-conditioning shed, and Doc and Dalton were gone.

Charlotte said she and her mother were out of money and putting Pallas's expenses on a credit card. They would have to sell her. Charlotte's mother was a flight attendant who flew from Burbank to Hawaii and back three times a week.

"I can give her up," said Charlotte. "We have to. I know that. But that will be a hard day. We went to Del Mar. We went to City of Industry. We went to Indio, Micah."

"How did you learn to ride so well?"

"I made my legs strong," she said. "I don't know what she'll think when I don't come around anymore."

Micah put his arm around her and she leaned her head on his shoulder. "I'm never having a credit card," he said.

"It's too much," she said. "The vet, the board, the feed, the farrier."

She slid away and lay down with her head on Micah's thigh. "Pallas Athena was almost Horse of the Year," she said quietly. "This is comfortable."

After a little while Micah said her name but she was asleep. He laced his fingers behind his head and lay back on the roof of the shed. "I'm up on a tightrope," someone sang below. Micah wondered what Tiny would say about a girl who was sad because she might have to give up her jumping horse. He might not make fun of her if he knew she was Micah's friend. He wondered where Indio was.

The way Charlotte said the name, it sounded like an enchanted city with streets paved in jade.

The woman in the long red shirt woke them up. The party was over, the night cold. Charlotte sat up and rested her head in her hands with closed eyes. The leg she'd used for a pillow was dead to feeling and Micah hobbled around until he was ready to go.

Five or six times a year Joan visited a fortune-teller named Dijkstra in the desert. He lived on a long gravel road off Old Woman Springs Road north of Twentynine Palms Highway in the isolated beauty of that country.

Much as she loved the Joshua trees and the high desert, Joan could not have lived alone here as Dijkstra did. The darkness would close around her—she would be out of her mind in a matter of days.

Dijkstra's house was three stories tall and the paint had been peeled away by the wind. Dusty velvet curtains moved in the windows, ceramics lined the sills. The place looked like something from an old photograph but for a satellite dish off to the side.

Dijkstra made pottery that he sold in the towns along the highway, and he used the potter's wheel for divination as well.

He met her at the front door. In his seventies, he wore a pith helmet, khaki shirt and shorts, light green socks up to his knees, and battered desert boots.

Years ago he'd been a marine researcher in Monterey, but one day he got the bends while diving and in the recompression chamber received a vision of living in the desert.

They went into the kitchen and sat on opposite sides of the potter's wheel. Beside the wheel a cactus grew in a terra-cotta pot, and the Palm Springs Yellow Pages lay on the wooden floor.

"How are things?" said Dijkstra.

"I got a role in a movie, and my son came to live with us," said Joan. "He's fourteen and doing pretty well, I think—he's made friends, got on the volleyball team at school. The other night he didn't come home till three in the morning."

"You must have been worried."

"I was asleep. He came in and woke me up. I can't stay mad at him. I can't even *get* mad at him. I was out of his life for a long time."

"This happens with families."

Dijkstra picked up the Yellow Pages and handed them to Joan. She let the book fall open in her lap. She tore out a page and placed it on the wheel for the turning of clay.

Dijkstra secured the page with Scotch tape. "Think back to the night your son woke you up. The transition from sleep is a time when insight is strongest."

"Okay. Doing that."

He placed his hands on his knees and worked a foot treadle. The potter's wheel began to turn, and the right angles of the page gave way to a circle spinning on the wheel.

"This is the part we don't like so much, said Dijkstra."

"It hurts," said Joan.

"What is pain?"

She remembered the night. The bedroom door creaked, Micah said he was home. Joan got out of bed and they went into the hallway and she held his arms and looked into his eyes. The part of the mother will be played this evening by Joan Gower. Micah's eyes were the innocent cinnamon color they always were.

Now she pricked her finger on a cactus thorn, and holding her hand over the wheel she squeezed out a drop of blood that fell to the spinning page, a dark blot dissolving in motion.

"You did that very well," said Dijkstra.

He left off pedaling and watched the wheel as it slowed and stopped. Joan pressed her fingertip to her teeth. The blood had made a nebula pattern among the names and numbers that the fortune-teller examined with a magnifying glass.

"You will sleep with a man in a small house," he said. "There is forest all around. You don't know how you feel about him."

"Oh wait, I know what that is. The plot of the movie I'm going to be in. Very good."

"As for your son, he will be a good volleyball player, and many people will come to see him play. But when you see him play, that game he will lose."

"That's not fair. Maybe I should stay away."

Dijkstra set the magnifying glass on the wheel. He put a drop of Neosporin on Joan's fingertip and wrapped it with a Band-Aid.

"Perhaps you could go to a game that is not critical in the standings."

"I hate to be the cause of him losing."

"You're not. It's the way it happens. You won't avoid seeing it, he won't avoid losing."

"What else?"

"You should be careful about this movie role. It might be tempting to leave television, but maybe that's not the best way to go."

"Is that in the blood?"

"Not really," he said. "I'm just thinking of television actors who have tried to make that transition and ended up neither here nor there. And there is a young woman. Help me. Around your son."

"That's probably Charlotte."

"She is important to him."

"Mmm. Already."

"He will fight for her."

"Will she break his heart?"

"She's his first love. What else would she do? But you just have to let that go. He has more wisdom than you might think."

"I knew it."

Joan rubbed her bandaged finger and asked how Dijkstra's investments were doing. Besides making pottery and telling fortunes he traded stocks on a computer in the living room.

"I try not to hold anything more than three days," he said. "The whole thing could go over at any time."

Joan drove back to the city through fields of windmills. She knew better than to explain Dijkstra's method to people because the blood part would seem weird, but it made sense to her, requiring more input from the sitter than Tarot or palmistry, which people had no problem with.

CHAPTER EIGHT

A MAN hired Tiny Darling to pull the seats out of the old Trinity Church in Grafton. The church had shut down years back and the little congregation had moved on to Sunday services in Chesley or Stone City. Some had stopped going at all.

The man had come up from Morrisville with the thought of remodeling the church and renting it out as housing. He wanted to make his reputation as the one who saves old churches by turning them into apartments.

"That'll never happen," said Tiny, "but whatever you say."

"You're not looking ahead."

"There's houses going empty in this town. And that's houses."

"Aha. This is not a house, it's a church. Prices are rising in Morrisville and Stone City. Where will people go?"

"They say Texas is popular."

"I will call it the Trinity Apartments."

"Here's what I'll do on the chairs," said Tiny. "Ten dollars apiece."

"Five."

"Seven," said Tiny

"Done."

It was cold and dark inside the church. Water stains streaked the walls, the rugs had turned to threads, birds had built nests between the ceiling beams.

The chairs were made of bentwood and black iron and joined in rows of eight on either side of the aisle. They'd come from a movie theater in Chicago about a hundred years ago.

The legs were fixed to the floor with bolts petrified by time and rust. But Tiny had wrenches and ratchets and pipes, and every bolt gives up some way. As he worked he thought about the Trinity. The Holy Ghost always seemed like the wild card. What was his job? Tiny was not sure.

He rigged a plywood ramp down the stairs and dragged the chairs out and loaded them on a flatbed truck. They'd go to the landfill except for four he set aside to put on his back porch.

Church chairs at Tiny's house would be something to talk about, should anyone show up in the mood for conversation.

At noon he pulled his gloves off, got his lunch from the cab of the truck, and sat in the churchyard eating and drinking a beer.

Louise's mother came along the sidewalk with her walking stick. Mary Montrose had gotten small these days. She wouldn't like him drinking beer in the shade of the church but she only asked what he was doing.

Tiny pushed one of the wooden seats down for Mary. It was a hot day and his neck and shoulders felt strong and useful from the pulling and dragging.

"I'd live in a tent before I took an apartment in that building," Mary said. "They say thousands of bats come flying out of the steeple at night."

Tiny reconsidered the nests he'd seen. He didn't know how bats lived. Thousands seemed a high estimate. He gave the beer can a shake, tipped it up, put it in the paper sack.

"It's rough inside, I can tell you that."

"If it can't be a church, I'd just as soon let it go," said Mary. "I remember Louise and June standing on the stage saying their pieces at Christmas Eve."

June was Mary's other daughter, a year or two older than Louise. She lived out West, in Colorado if she hadn't moved, and didn't come home much anymore.

"Far as that goes, Louise and Dan Norman got married in there, didn't they?"

Mary nodded.

"Once she'd divorced me."

Mary had an old person's look in her eyes, as if the view from the churchyard was unlike anything she'd ever seen. "You and Louise were not married."

This was not necessarily senility on Mary's part. She had hardly acknowledged the marriage when it was on.

"The way those girls would laugh in church," she said. "They had their own words to the songs."

"Like what?"

"Let me think," said Mary. "Do you know the song 'Make Me a Blessing'?"

"No."

"Well, there is such a song. But they would say 'make me a sandwich.'"

"Oh. That is kind of funny."

"They thought so. And they would try not to laugh out loud but that only made it worse. Their shoulders would get to shaking, and pretty soon you could feel it all down the row. The minister hated us. They were just high-spirited girls."

"I saw Louise the other day," said Tiny. "She was washing her truck with a chamois. I was too married to her."

"You believe what you want to believe."

Tiny helped Mary get up, gave her the walking stick, and watched her make her uncertain way across the grass. How much longer would she go on? Tiny wondered. Or his own mother? It was hard to picture the world without them. After a bad storm the sky sometimes appeared a paler blue, too frail to hold up the sun. Maybe it would be something like that.

*   *   *

End of the day, the job half done: a grid of pale ovals on the floor marked his progress, showing where the legs of the chairs had been bolted down.

Tiny drove the flatbed to the landfill off the Mixerton Road north of the Rust River. He loved the landfill. It felt like another country —the bulldozers and the burial mounds they made, the sound and the dust, the swarms of birds.

He parked and stepped into the doorway of a corrugated building. The supervisor looked up from a fishing magazine.

"And what do we have today, Tiny?"

He came out to see the chairs in case they were something the landfill workers could use, but on consideration they had chairs enough.

Tiny drove along the ridge road. A bulldozer climbed a mountain of dirt and refuse. Fertilizer sacks darted in the wind like ghosts at Halloween.

Tiny stopped the truck and ran the lift. The church seats clung to the bed till it was pitched too steep and then they began to scrape and slide to the ground.

One night Louise drove through a thunderstorm to see a woman named Marian about a clock. She lived in Dogwood Crescent, a fancy neighborhood on the west side of Stone City. Louise parked the Scout beside a tall brick house with electric candles shining in bands of windows.

Louise never owned an umbrella, as she associated them with old people, so she ran across the street holding a newspaper over her head. Lightning turned the street white, and then came the thunder.

The woman Marian answered the door. She had blue eye shadow and long silver hair and she wore a red kimono with white lilies. Louise stood bedraggled and dripping in the entrance.

"I'm Louise, from the shop," she said.

"Britt," called Marian.

A younger man came to the front of the house in a white turtle-neck sweater and burgundy jacket. His slippers were black with gold medallions.

"Take the lady's newspaper and coat. She's come about the clock."

"Oh, very good."

Britt took the newspaper from Louise and read the headlines. "Teens kidnapped at gunpoint, forced to drive man across town," he said.

"Is this the time to be reading the news? Where are your manners? Are you hungry, Louise? My son is a chef."

"You sent me a photograph of a clock," said Louise.

"So I did," said the mother. "Make Louise something to eat, Britt. In the meantime I will take her to see the clock."

It was on a desk in an alcove with a heating grate by the living room. The base housed a garden scene in which two girls rode swings, tiny porcelain hands holding the wires, one girl swinging forward as the other swung back. The case was mahogany with gold inlay. A trellis laced with tiny roses formed an arch over the swings.

"When was it made?" said Louise.

"Oh I wouldn't know. The thirties or forties I should think. It belonged to my aunt."

"Why are you selling it?"

"I've grown tired of hearing it tick. I suppose that's an odd reason, but these things happen. And Britt doesn't care for it either."

Britt stepped into the alcove. "No, the clock, I hate it," he said. "Please come eat while it's hot."

The kitchen had a fireplace with a fire going. Britt had set the table for one—a bowl of soup, a basket of homemade bread, red wine in a proper glass. Louise didn't understand why they were making such a production out of selling a clock.

She spread a pressed white napkin in her lap. Steam rose from the bowl. Britt and Marian sat on either side of Louise, watching her intently. She picked up the spoon and tried the soup.

"Good God, this is excellent," said Louise.

"What did I say, Britt?" said Marian. "Britt lacks confidence."

"Jesus," said Britt. "You don't have to tell her that."

Louise tore a piece of the bread, dipped it in the soup. She took a drink of the wine. "Now, about the clock," she said. "I'm not sure I can give you what it's worth."

"We will not talk money at the table," said Marian.

Louise figured she would keep the clock, having acquired it with so much ceremony. Dan met her at the door of the farmhouse.

"I was beginning to think I lost you," he said.

"Is the house leaking?"

"Just that corner where it always does. I put a bucket down."

"Look what I have."

They took the clock up to the bedroom and Louise set it on the dresser and plugged it in. With her finger she gave one of the children a push to get them swinging.

Dan leaned his arms on the dresser and studied the clock. He found a thin red button on the side and pushed it. A bulb hidden behind the trellis lit the painted girls on the swings.

"Will the ticking bother you?" Louise asked.

"No. Will the light bother you?"

"Yes."

"We can turn the light off."

And she understood this as a kindness, because Dan loved the small and incidental lighting of appliances, clocks, radios in the dark. Louise thought this might have something to do with memories of the sheriff's cruisers and their busy dashboards.

Her hair was wet from the rain and she dried it with a towel and then sat in a white nightgown brushing her hair at the bureau.

They could hear the wind and rain and the clock. When she came to bed she was all over him like a shadow.

Jack Snow drove home from the Little Fox, an old-style strip club that suited his taste in sexual exhibitionism. Pole dancing he didn't care for. It looked more like work than dancing.

At Wendy's place he found that his key no longer opened the door. He knocked and knocked. Rain hammered the roof and over-flowed the gutter, making curtains of water around the porch.

Wendy came to the living room window. She held a phone and dialed. Jack's phone rang. They talked with the window glass between them. Her lips moved and a little time passed while the signal traveled from the living room to wherever it went and back to the porch.

"You can't live here anymore, Jack. Your things are in the garage. We're done. I'm sorry it's such a rotten night, but the locksmith came today, and I don't make the weather."

"What is this about?"

Her phone flashed red. "Hold, please. I'm getting another call."

She sat on the arm of the couch and covered her mouth with her hand.

"That's my dad. He wants to know should he come over and make you go. He doesn't mind."

"Look at me. I'm standing in the rain."

"What should I tell him? He's on hold."

"I'll go. What else would I do?"

"When?"

"However long it takes to load the car."

"All right. One second please."

There was standing water on the porch, and Jack walked around on his heels to keep the leather of his shoes from getting soaked.

"Okay," said Wendy. "He's on his way over."

"What'd I just say?"

"He doesn't trust you. I don't think anyone ever did trust you but me, Jackie. And even I didn't, very much."

"What happened? Why are you doing this?"

"They're watching you. They know what you're doing. My parents hired the sheriff. Well, he used to be the sheriff. He investigated you."

"What I'm doing? What we're doing."

"That's the other thing. I quit. Why didn't you tell me you were in prison?"

"Hey. A lot of people are in prison. At least open the door and say goodbye."

"That's what my dad said you would say."

"You're making a mistake. The business is about to take off."

"You should take off."

Jack backed the Mustang into the garage, where he found three boxes on the concrete floor. Opening them to make sure she hadn't kept his music system, he saw that she had baked him a pie, wrapped it in wax paper, and laid it on top of his shoes and moccasins. He took the pie out and placed it on the floor, determined not to take her charity. But it looked good, so he put it back in the box.

He loaded the trunk and closed the lid and tried the key to the door in the garage.

"Not this one either," said Wendy from the other side.

"Thanks for the pie," said Jack.

"Oh. You're welcome. It's apple."

"Hey, Wendy."

"What?"

"Remember when I said you were smart?"

"No."

"Well, I'm not so sure about that anymore. I think you might have a learning disorder."

"You don't scare me."

Jack power-braked in front of the duplex. Smoke rolled from the burning tires in the rain. If she was watching at all she would only find this comical or sad. He took his foot off the brake and the Mustang bolted.

"Ain't my night," he said.

Perhaps his car would spin out and crash into her father's car coming the other way. A fiery collision. How ironic that would be. But Jack didn't want to die. That was the problem in that scenario.

He went up to the trainyard and carried the boxes into the warehouse. He sat in the office eating apple pie and drinking whiskey. Later he made a bed of packing quilts and fell asleep next to the catalytic heater.

The crow rescued by Louise from the street only to die days later came back to the thrift store. It happened in a roundabout way.

Roman Baker, the father of the twin vets, was retired and often came to the animal hospital to sit in the waiting room.

He would read magazines, do crosswords, look out the window, watch the reaction of dogs when they realized there were cats inside cat carriers.

The twins weren't happy about his hanging around but they could hardly object as he was their father and still owned the building.

When the crow died the old man decided that it should be stuffed and mounted and given to Louise. The twins disagreed, saying she might not appreciate the gesture.

He went ahead, enlisting the services of a locally famous taxidermist who had his own radio show and agreed to do the work at cost.

When the crow was finished the twin Roman Jr. said he would take it to Louise. He'd had a crush on her since he was fourteen and she was in her early thirties. He was almost thirty now himself and had two children but remembered how the image of Louise haunted his younger years. He would probably run off with her today. Not that he would ask or she would say yes. Just something to dream about.

A sign on the thrift shop door said Louise would be back at two-thirty. Roman Jr. sat down on the steps with the crow in an ungainly package of brown paper.

In a little while Louise pulled up riding a powder-blue motor scooter. She put the kickstand down and took off a black helmet. She shook her head and her red hair fell to the shoulders of a Morrisville-Wylie letter jacket.

"What's that?" said Roman Jr.

"A Vespa. Someone wants to sell it to me so I thought I should know how it works. I like it."

"I've got something for you."

She sat beside him with the helmet at her feet. "If this keeps up I will be in the Fortune 500."

Roman handed her the package.

"Now, this was our dad's idea," he said. "He's always looking for something to do. Anyway, remember how hard you took it when that crow died?"

"It bothered me. Yeah."

"Anyway, Dad knows this taxidermist, he's got a show on the radio."

"Oh Jesus, Roman. Not the crow."

"Well, no, it is. It is the crow."

"Will I want to see it?"

"I don't know. I'll take it and hide it somewhere if you don't want it."

Louise unwrapped the package. The crow stood on driftwood, feathers interlaced and smooth. The beak pointed down and to the side, as if the crow were listening intently to sounds of the wild.

"It does look natural," said Louise.

"Yeah. The guy does a hell of a job."

"Please thank your dad for me."

Louise put the crow in the shop window on a wooden table engraved with sunflowers, where it remains to this day. She hung a tag on it saying I'M NOT FOR SALE.

On Saturday mornings Lyris would drive out to the Red Robin Bakery for cinnamon rolls and coffee and bring them back to Louise's store.

She imagined that the people at the bakery would get to know her, saying, "I wonder where Lyris is this morning. I'm sure she'll be here any minute to pick up her cinnamon rolls."

Lyris drove back to town with the coffee and the rolls. The coffee cups were in a cardboard holder made for four cups. If you only had two cups you had to wedge them in diagonally across from each other—if they were placed on the same side the holder would tip over every time.

Lyris and Louise stood at the counter drinking coffee and pulling the rolls into strips. "I see you have a crow now."

"A weird story," said Louise.

She told it, from the day the bus hit the crow and the strange customer came in to the day Roman Jr. turned up with the package.

"You said a tall woman," said Lyris.

"Could have reached anything in the store without a ladder."

"Albert tried to interview a woman a while ago. Said she was really tall."

"What was her name?"

"I forget. She had white hair."

"Platinum," said Louise. "Was she trying to find a rock?"

"I don't know."

"This one was."

"The interview fell apart. She attacked a bartender with a yardstick."

"That you do not do."

"He tried to take it from her. She hit Albert too."

"This must have been some interview."

That afternoon Louise dyed Lyris's hair magenta in the back room. Lyris sat on a wooden chair wearing a white plastic bonnet that made her look like a pilgrim maiden. Louise stood behind her with a crochet hook drawing locks of hair through small holes in the bonnet so that some hair would get the dye and some wouldn't.

As Louise worked they watched a documentary about the Ouija board on an old Admiral television set with rabbit ears.

"Of course the thing moves," said Louise. "People's hands are on it."

"I used to know somebody who was good at the Ouija board," said Lyris. "It scared me. The staff at the orphanage would pay her to tell them things."

Louise worked the dye into Lyris's hair. "Like what?"

"This one guy, he was an electrician, he lost his wedding ring, and she said where to find it."

"I know. A motel."

Lyris laughed. "No," she said. "Behind the sink."

"Sometimes it seems like you thought the orphanage was okay."

"It was the Four Seasons compared to the foster homes."

After letting the dye soak in for twenty minutes, Louise wrestled the bonnet from Lyris's head, washed her hair in the sink, and dried it with a heavy avocado-colored blow-dryer from the store. They looked at her hair, a lovely mix of brunette and wine red, in the mirror above the sink.

"I believe you are the prettiest girl in town," said Louise.

CHAPTER NINE

THE SCREENWRITER for *The Powder Horn* asked for a meeting with Joan, as he had admired her audition reel and wanted to talk about her scenes.

On the appointed day Joan drove into the wilds above Malibu to a property guarded by a chain-link gate. She parked her silver car and walked around the fence and up a soft trail in the shadows of the trees. She'd read of skeletons discovered in the canyons, remains of persons unknown or missing for years.

A short walk brought her to a cabin with walls of rough rails, small dusty windows, and a steep and mossy roof. It was surrounded at some distance by a crooked picket fence, missing paint and slats, and she walked through the gate and sat down on the steps.

The screenwriter came along after a bit, wearing a flat cap and summer suit of lightweight tweed, one hand in his pocket and the other idly tapping the points of the fence.

"This belonged to a studio called Pinnacle Pictures in the forties," he said. "They made *The Cattle Raid* and *Past Ruined Abilene* here. This is the cabin I had in mind as I wrote so I thought it would be a good place for us to talk. I hope it's no trouble."

Joan picked up a pine needle and rolled it between her fingers, enjoying the tackiness of the sap. "It helps me understand Ann Flowers."

The screenwriter removed his cap and ran a hand over his dark and wavy hair. "You helped *me* understand Ann Flowers," he said. "I've watched your reading a hundred times."

"Hmm," said Joan. "That's too many."

"There is a power in it."

"That's like *The Ring*."

He looked at her with large and melancholy eyes. "What were you thinking of?"

"When?"

"In the reading."

"How alone she is," said Joan. "How her life changed because of a memory. Which she's probably forgotten, on the surface."

"I think she has forgotten."

"But all the same, it's there. The way things are for everyone."

"Let's go inside."

He took a key ring from his pocket and unlocked the door. The cabin had a farm table, a fireplace, and a sleigh bed with a red quilt. It was dark and musty and cool.

"Do you know why I asked you here?" said the screenwriter.

"It was foretold by a man in the desert."

"He mentioned me?"

"It was more general. A man. A cabin."

"So what happens?"

"That would be a little easy," said Joan. "What do you want to happen?"

"Well, you know. Take you in my arms. Kiss you. Get back what is lost."

"Like Ann Flowers and Davy."

"Is that it? Maybe that is it."

Joan moved close to him. His deep and transparent sadness excited her. She had a thing for the troubled ones. The blood rose to her face and she felt the heat pulse beneath her eyes. She kissed the screenwriter on the mouth. "That is what happens," she said.

They spent the afternoon in the cabin bed and then took a walk in the forest. The screenwriter, whose name was Gray, said there had been a zoo of exotic animals on the grounds until the fifties, when many escaped and it was shut down.

*   *   *

A few days later Joan visited a clothes shop called Hazmat on Robertson Boulevard. There was a stone Buddha in a black marble fountain, and music played softly, French women singing in English and in French. The saleswomen stood prettily around the shop, sleek and alert.

Joan took a dress into the dressing room which was large with green wallpaper and a wicker couch and bottled black tea. She put the dress on and looked in the mirror, shifting her shoulders, putting one leg forward, then the other. Someone knocked on the door. Joan opened it a little and there was Gray holding a pair of fawn ankle boots.

"Are you following me?" she said.

"Yeah, pretty much. Try these on."

She sat on the couch and Gray knelt like a shoe salesman slipping her feet into the soft boots and zipping them up the sides. He wore a double-breasted cotton suit of light blue. Joan thought he must make a lot of money.

"When do you write?" she said.

"At night."

"Are you crazy?"

"Not clinically. See how they feel."

Joan's natural curiosity about the fit of the boots overrode her urge to send him from the room and from her life. She got up and walked around.

"Do you like this dress?" she said.

He pulled her close and kissed her.

"Oh, Gray," said Joan. "Will this be the last time?"

"Yes."

"Promise?"

"Never again."

She took the dress off and put it sadly on the hanger.

"Not one sound," she whispered.

He thought she should sit on the couch but she took him by the lapels and laid him on the floor. She wanted to mess up his precious clothes. She saw herself in the mirror, hands on his arms. She looked like no one she knew, and the sense of there being someone else in her place made her come so hard it scared her.

Joan dried her eyes with the tissues thoughtfully provided by Hazmat, and they got dressed and left together. She bought the dress, a normal thing to do; people bought dresses all the time. Her credit card she offered with both hands to keep it from shaking.

The affair, though Joan told herself it did not really qualify, made her avid for family life. She would sit with Rob on the couch, legs tucked warmly beneath her, watching the football games and horror films that he loved above all other entertainments.

Joan knew little about football and usually couldn't tell who had the ball or where it was on the field. She liked the referees, their jailhouse shirts and loud voices that filled the stadiums without visible amplification, reminding her of Vavoom from the *Felix the Cat* cartoons.

The horror movies gave her nightmares in which the monsters she killed would never stay dead. She would shoot or stab them to no avail. She came to feel sorry for the relentless creatures that, after all, her mind had created.

Rob studied the scenes for blank areas from which the bad surprise would emerge. He would lean forward, pointing. "Watch right here," he would say.

He didn't take the action seriously no matter how gross it became and would sometimes laugh as if watching a family film. He was a strange man in some ways. She knew he was glad to have her beside him by the way he would reach out and touch her hair.

What would he say if he knew that she'd had sex with a screenwriter in a whispery dress shop on Robertson? Had that really happened? Safe at home it seemed imaginary.

She helped Micah with his homework, with which he was over-whelmed. He had to do math and science and English and Spanish, to read *The Turn of the Screw,* to memorize the presidents in order. He and Joan came up with a mnemonic trick they called "The Age of Fabric" for a string of obscure presidents whose names suggested things that could be done to cloth: Tyler, Polk, Taylor, Fillmore, Pierce.

Before going to bed, Joan would stop at Eamon's door. He never seemed to be doing homework. At Deep Rock Academy senior year seemed a time for reflection and smoking weed. He would be playing the mandolin or talking on the phone. Joan would ask him to do "Puff, the Magic Dragon." A children's song, she knew, but it always grieved her when Jackie Paper came no more.

Gray did not keep his promise. He turned up one day when Joan was alone at home, having just made a volleyball court for Micah on the back lawn.

It was more work than she'd expected. She laid it out with strings and stakes, poured bright white court lines from a bag of lime. The net sagged when first put up, so she took it down and started over.

It was two-thirty when she finished. She went inside and made a gin and tonic and came back out to sit in a lawn chair. It was a volleyball court to be proud of, net taut and bordered by white tape between stout blue poles tethered to the ground. The sun had moved beyond the house, and sweat dried on her skin.

That's when the screenwriter opened the lattice gate and walked into the yard. He wore gabardines, a batik shirt, leather shoes with basket-weave insets.

"No, no, no, no, no," said Joan. "You do not come here."

"I wanted to see where you live."

"Shut up. Get out of my yard."

He got down on his knees and put his arms around her legs, speaking into the front of her jeans. She couldn't hear what he was saying, could only feel the vibrations through the zipper.

She bumped the side of his head with the hand that held the drink.

"Gray," she said.

"What?"

"Get up, now. Have my drink."

He stood and finished the gin and tonic. "I think it's time we spoke to your husband."

Joan took the empty glass, tossed it on the lawn, and hit him in the face. This seemed to have no effect. He kept looking at her with his deerlike eyes.

"It's the honorable thing."

"There is something wrong with you, Gray. Something serious. Now I'm going in the house. I will not see you again. You will not see me again."

She locked the door and watched him from inside. He stood for a moment and then turned and walked through the gate, latching it on the way out.

"And I thought, you know, one time, what's the harm," said Joan. "Isn't that how men are supposed to be?"

She and Paige England were having Irish coffee at El Camino in Los Feliz. Paige was the star of *Forensic Mystic*. She went everywhere with a red spaniel named Jim, and El Camino allowed dogs.

"Men have changed," said Paige. "You can't count on them to be callous and evasive anymore."

"But this one is just nuts."

"Have you lost weight?"

"Do I look unwell?" said Joan.

"You look beautiful and unwell. Like someone with tuberculosis."

"I'm just hoping this doesn't mess me up in the film."

Paige waved her hand. "If sex messed up films, nothing would ever get made."

She had white hair worn in ringlets. She'd gotten into acting playing the teenaged daughter of a dockworker in *Bay of Smokes* in the seventies. The director came from Belgium and never made another film in the United States. It was a cult favorite.

"I think they're writing me out of *Forensic*," said Joan.

"It's nothing I've heard."

"But you would tell me if you did."

Paige took a drink. "Yes. Absolutely."

Her dog got up, barked, turned in a circle, and lay down again.

"Jim smells a coyote," said Paige.

Micah and Thea had her house to themselves except for an artist named Donald who was said to be painting the walls of some distant wing.

Thea's father was sailing around Catalina, her mother was gardening, and her brother was in Madrid playing the oboe with an orchestra.

Thea had been banned from the treehouse after her parents found the weed tin. There was a padlock on the door.

They went upstairs. Paintings of lords and ladies lounging about in nature lined the stairwell. They held things in their hands—a pear, a bird, a magnifying glass. The steps creaked and the subjects of the paintings seemed to watch them with mild suspicion.

Thea took plates of melon and lemon from a refrigerator in her room and they sat eating by the windows looking out on the green blades of a palm tree.

Micah twisted in his chair and bit his upper lip.

"What's wrong?"

"The sound. Forks on plates. It makes me want to get up and walk around."

"We can go bother Donald."

The painter was in a hallway on the third floor with tables and chairs covered in drop cloths. He sponged red and gold paint on the walls while a radio played classical music.

"Thea," he said mockingly. He wore white coveralls, a gold earring, and a blue handkerchief on his head.

"Donald."

"I won't be watched."

"We are fascinated by your stippling."

"Go outside. Run like the wind."

"Mom said we could be inside."

"Not in here, little ones."

"Micah is taller than you."

Finally they went back to Thea's room and lay on the bed with their heads at opposite ends.

"You have strange toes," said Micah.

"Why, thank you."

"Like little soldiers on a hill."

Thea sat up on her elbows to look at her feet. "Do they seem different than other toes?"

"Yours are the only ones I've studied."

"Take your socks off."

"You don't want to see my feet."

"Take them off. You made fun of mine."

Micah sat up, took his socks off, and showed her his broken toes. "This one I tripped on the stairs and it bent back," he said. "This one I was walking on the rail and fell off and jammed it on a cross tie."

"Did it hurt?"

"Oh yeah. It even bled. Inside and out."

"You should never walk on railroad tracks. People get killed."

"The train don't go through anymore," said Micah. "Weeds are growing up through the tracks."

"Oh well, the changing face of America," said Thea. "Charlotte said you kissed."

"What about it?"

"Was it good?"

"Yeah."

"I bet. And what else?"

"Nothing else."

"You would like something else."

Micah turned on his side, looking past Thea's feet at a poster of Akira walking down to his red motorcycle.

"I wouldn't know where to begin," he said.

"Yes."

"Do you feel that way?"

"Definitely," said Thea.

"I mean, where to *begin*."

"But then what," said Thea. "Then what."

"And they say the first time might not be that great."

"I've heard that, too."

"Maybe you could skip the first time and go right to the second time."

"Or you'll know when the time is right," said Thea. "Which sounds good, but I'm not sure that you would know. Or the time might be right for one person when, for the other person, umm, actually, the time could be better."

"You can't overthink it."

"Would you kiss me?" said Thea.

"If the time was right."

She laughed and threw a pillow at him.

"Are you out of your mind?" she said. "I don't want you to kiss me."

After a while Charlotte came over and picked up Thea and Micah, and they headed for Micah's house to play volleyball on the new court.

On the way they saw a Phamish truck parked on the street. They stood in line on the sidewalk beside an old movie theater with faded red letters stuck randomly on the marquee.

They got banh mi sandwiches and sat on the tailgate of Charlotte's pickup eating in the shade of a tree that grew from a hole in the sidewalk.

Micah said he liked how you could go places in Los Angeles and find good food for a few dollars and you didn't have to sit around waiting for it and they handed it out the window of a truck.

"Micah hates forks and plates," said Thea.

"This is Los Angeles," said Charlotte.

They played volleyball till the sun went down. The lines Joan had made in the grass glowed brighter and brighter in the dark. Then it got too cold and they went into the house, where Joan had laid out food on the dining room table. They loaded their plates and ate in the TV room. There was a fire in the fireplace and the television played a football game with the sound turned down.

Rob talked of the old days of the Los Angeles Rams when they played at the Coliseum with a bunch of players none of the others had heard of. But the names had a legendary sound and Joan and the teenagers listened and understood a little of what those days meant to him.

CHAPTER TEN

I FEEL like I could talk all night," said Louise. "I feel like having some grapes. Would you like some grapes?"

"What?" said Dan.

"Would you like some grapes?"

"What time is it?"

"Quarter to three," Louise said. "I took cold medicine."

Dan sat up. "If we're going to have grapes, I would have a grilled cheese sandwich."

They put on their robes and tied them tight against the cold and Louise followed Dan down the stairs with her hands on his shoulders, steering his sleepy body.

Louise paused on the landing. "Do you know how it is when you're awake, and you try to wake the other person up, but you know they're not going to? And you're alone in the world with your nighttime worries and the morning far away."

Dan reached back and laid his hand on top of hers and they continued down the stairs.

He turned on the counter light and stood motionless for a moment, then took a loaf of bread from the cupboard and Swiss cheese and mustard from the refrigerator.

"Would you like a grilled cheese?"

"That's okay," said Louise.

She sat at the table picking green grapes from a wooden bowl.

Dan heated a square black skillet and put the sandwich on and covered it with the lid of a saucepan. He stood by the windows running water into a glass.

"Are you seeing this?" he said.

She had been looking at him but only then did she notice the giant snowflakes sliding like paper against the glass.

"Do you remember how you would have to go out on nights like this?"

"I do."

"There's a three-car pileup. A fire. A domestic," said Louise. "You'd better flip your sandwich, love."

Dan lifted the lid and turned the sandwich over. He knit his fingers behind his neck and yawned. He had an extreme yawn, like that of a TV lion on the veldt.

"And you'd go out in your nightgown and boots to warm up the cruiser," he said.

She put a grape in her mouth and sliced it clean down the middle with her front teeth. "I did, didn't I? Sometimes I did."

Dan sliced the grilled cheese on the diagonal and brought it to the table. He missed a little more of his sideburns every time he shaved and was beginning to look like someone in a Western.

"What are your nighttime worries?" he said.

"There's so many," she said. "That I haven't been kind. That there's a meanness in me. That we will die."

"The last part is the only true one."

"Do you look at the obituaries? People are living older and older, but they're also dying younger and younger."

"I know what you mean."

"Then we'll be done, and they'll sell our house, and it will be like we were never here. I think of the people that will buy our house. I can see them walking from room to room, thinking 'Oh, we can do way better than those other people did.' You know, like everyone does when they look at a house. Do you worry about that?"

"Not till you said it," said Dan. "We probably have thirty years anyway. Maybe more. I could see us being really old. Think how many things will happen in that time."

"Like what?"

"I don't know. People going to the moon on vacation."

"Would you go the moon? I don't think I would."

"Well, if they fixed it up a little bit."

"I think I'm bothering Lyris and Albert."

"Did they say that?"

"No."

"I think they would. They're not shy people."

"They are, though," said Louise. "You don't know them like I do. One night I got mixed up and said I was her mother."

"I wouldn't fault you for that."

"I just wish we had our girl," whispered Louise.

Dan nodded, breathing quietly.

"Then she could have the house. And she could be running through it, and someday her kids could be running through it. And we would say, 'Slow down, you're going to hurt yourself.'"

She laid her head on her arms.

"This is what the night does," she said. "Puts sad things in your mind."

Reading the newspaper one day Tiny Darling happened on an article about a man who got caught trying to rob the Big Wonder store in Morrisville.

Big Wonder had come in ten years ago, one of the land-eating flat stores that killed off town businesses for miles around. No one who worked there seemed to have the least idea of what was in the store, how it worked, or where to find it. They wandered around in green smocks trying to avoid contact with customers.

The robber's plan was clever up to a point. He hid in an expedition tent in the sporting goods pavilion until the middle of the night. Police said he picked up a *Field & Stream* magazine in the store that he read to while away the hours. Then he came out of the tent and crawled to the video counter.

Tiny doubted that part. It would be an absurdly long crawl. Two guards caught the man and held him at gunpoint till the cops came. What fun it must have been for the guards to pull their guns. They were going to get a plaque for their good service.

The thief had approached the problem from the wrong perspective. He'd fixated on getting into the store after hours, when the more important question was how to get out.

And so Tiny drove over to Morrisville one night. Big Wonder was on the south side of Highway 56 with an open field behind it and beyond that a housing development called The Foxglove.

Tiny parked on the edge of The Foxglove and surveyed the back of Big Wonder through binoculars. It was a mental exercise. He had nothing else to do with Micah gone. Moonlight glittered on the snow in the field. Tiny ran the car and listened to music on the radio.

A Big Wonder semi arrived at the loading dock around midnight. The truck took an hour to unload and leave. Then came a period of twenty minutes or so when the doors of the loading dock were open as night workers moved boxes around and came to the doorway every once in a while to smoke.

On the same night of the following week, Tiny returned. Once again the semi came, unloaded its cargo, and left. Tiny got out of his car and crossed the field, boots breaking crusted snow. It was a long walk. When he reached the loading bay, he picked up a large cardboard box, a wide-screen TV.

He walked back across the field, slid the TV into the backseat of the car, and got in the front. He took his gloves off and blew on his hands. From the dashboard he took a red Marks-A-Lot, uncapped it with his teeth, and wrote on the top of the box:

HEH, HEH

Then he drove out of The Foxglove, back to the highway, and around to the parking lot of Big Wonder. He stopped near the front doors, pulled the boxed TV from the backseat, leaned it against the glass, and drove home, where he made himself a drink.

To Tiny's surprise, his experimental raid on the flat store made the newspaper.

"We believe that the subject may have been laughing at the store, or possibly its security apparatus," said a Morrisville police lieutenant.

Tiny took the newspaper in both hands and gave it a shake. How he admired this lieutenant and his subtle criticism of Big Wonder.

The police did not think that the thief's initials were H.E.H., because there would be no reason to repeat them with a comma between.

Asked if the thief might fairly be called "the Laughing Bandit," the lieutenant said, "It's a free press. Call him whatever you want."

A blue van with tinted windows arrived one morning as Dan Norman cleared snow from the driveway at the farmhouse. He had an old orange Kubota with a front-end loader and four-foot scoop.

It was more tractor than you'd need for a driveway but he liked driving it because it reminded him of a tractor that the old farmer Henry Hamilton used to have, when there was a farm across the road and Henry lived on it. Dan would go into town and clear Louise's mother's driveway too.

Dan took the tractor out of gear, stepped on the brake, climbed down, and walked up the driveway through the drifts. The wind came up the hill from the south. His ears were warm in a wool Jones hat with the flaps down.

A man and a woman sat in the van wearing overcoats buttoned to the neck. The man rolled down the window.

"Morning," said Dan.

"Are you Dan Norman?"

He nodded.

"You know a man named Jack Snow?"

"Know of him. Who are you?"

"I'm Agent Sam Anders. This is Agent Betty Lee. We're with the federal government."

"It's good to have work these days."

The woman leaned toward the window. "How about you get in the vehicle and we go for a ride."

"I've got to finish plowing."

"We can wait."

"Well, yeah, but you'll have to move."

"I'll pull in," said the man.

"Ah, I don't know about that. It's pretty deep."

"This is four-wheel drive."

Agent Anders drove the van into snow up to the wheel wells and got stuck. Dan plowed a path to the van and hooked a chain on the chassis and pulled it out. He finished the driveway and waved for the agents to come into the house, where they sat in the kitchen while he made coffee.

"We want you to back off Jack Snow," said Agent Lee.

"I already have," said Dan. "That's done."

"What was it?"

"A family thing," said Dan.

"Wendy," said Agent Anders.

"We're not interested in Wendy," said Agent Lee. "We're investigating art theft. I'm from Justice, Sam's from Revenue. We've been observing Jack Snow since fall."

"That's how we know you were tailing him."

"Where were you?" said Dan.

"In the trainyard. A car on the siding."

"Isn't it cold?"

"We have a kerosene heater."

"They only do so much."

"Jack Snow is a small thing attached to a big thing. He's an associate of Andy from Omaha."

"He's the one you want."

"No. Andy's in Lons Ferry and will be for a long time. That's where he met Snow."

"We want his friends."

"I don't see where I can be of much use," said Dan. "Far as I know, Jack Snow's just fooling around with copies. Eating away at the metal. More of a hobby than a crime."

"That's what he thinks. But he's about to get something real. Then we'll have him."

"What is it?"

"It's a stone. Found in a bronze case in a bog in Ireland. A guy had it in his hands. They say he'd been dead a thousand years."

"How'd you come by it?" said Dan.

"We've never had it," said Agent Lee. "We're tracking it."

"And we're running out of time," said her partner.

Sandra Zulma took the county transit bus that ran from Stone City to Romyla along Highway 41. Besides herself on the bus there was an old couple with a small red and white dog in a green knitted sweater that sat looking out the window.

The highway went along the ridge and she could see the fields and the bare trees and the low places where water had pooled and frozen. It would not snow today.

Seeing the ranch house on the hill, Sandra pulled the cord to get off. A bell rang, the driver looked at her in the mirror, and she walked to the front of the bus holding the chrome rail. She lowered her head and pointed to the house.

Sandra got off the bus and walked up a long driveway banked high with snow. Her clothes were not suited to open country. She wore a wool suit jacket with the sleeves pulled down over her hands. She rapped on the storm door, and the glass bowed with a reflection of the bright and snowy yard.

Her cousin Terry came to the door, unshaved and wearing a flannel shirt and green down vest and gray sweatpants.

He'd always made her sad because he had been a smart child but he'd never figured out what to do with knowledge and so now he lived alone in a house with nothing around it.

"I didn't know who to expect, but I got to say it wasn't you," he said.

"I've come for Jack."

"Jack who?"

"Snow."

"Well, he ain't here but come on in."

Terry made hot chocolate and they carried their mugs into the living room, where heavy orange curtains made a dark warren of the room.

On the big television a figure skater leaped into the air and spun around and landed with a long and beautiful extension of limbs.

"God damn," said Terry. "That was a nice double axel. I've been watching this shit, it's really interesting. What do you want with Jack Snow?"

"We've got things to settle."

Terry found the clicker and turned off the TV. "He come by here about this time last year looking for a place to stay. I couldn't see what he'd ever done for me that I should put him up. Haven't seen him since that time. Well, that's not true, either. I seen him once in a bar, but I didn't go up to him. You know, I never liked the man personally. He's got some deal he runs out of a shed in the trainyard. You want my advice, Sandy, you forget about Jack Snow and go on home. Your mom and dad know where you are?"

Sandra drank her hot chocolate. "Not since I got out of the hospital."

"Well, I heard you were laid up."

"I was afraid."

"Of what?"

"Everything. I couldn't move. I couldn't eat. I'd go to sleep hoping I would never wake up and that would be best."

"You didn't mean it though."

"How you getting by, Terry?"

"Pretty good. I work half the year for Rex Construction. You wouldn't know them. Bridges and buildings and the like. I put a little money aside. This time of year I'm like an old bear. Ain't you got no winter clothes?"

"Just what I'm wearing."

"We can't have that."

Terry left the room and after a while came back dragging a big packing box across the orange shag carpet. He leaned into the box and began tossing out coats and boots and sweaters and mittens.

"These belonged to a girl I knew. She stayed with me a couple years ago. She was from Arkansas and I'm pretty sure that's where she went. Just left one summer day and I never heard of her again. Kind of miss her company. She was always talking about Little Rock. She's got some Rollerblades around here. I couldn't say where those are at the moment."

The clothes made her think she'd been meant to come. She outfitted herself with a knee-length Vikings sideline coat, an orange stocking cap with a tassel, a wool scarf, and a pair of cowled mittens with the Arctic Cat logo. She traded her shoes for heavy socks and Sorel boots with felt liners.

Terry drove Sandra back to Stone City in his truck. She was warm and happy. A hawk flew alongside the truck and turned away, wide and ragged wings beating against the sky. In town she directed Terry to the Continental Hotel.

"This where you're staying?" he said.

"I like it," she said. "And I like you, Terry."

She kissed him on the cheek.

"Go home, Sandy."

That night Tiny's mother went outside to burn the trash in the wire barrel in the backyard. The evergreens sagged with snow-laden branches in the dark. Shrouded in an Army surplus coat, she stuffed pages of newspaper through the wires and lit them.

She walked back to the birdbath in the yard and turned to watch the fire. It was a merry sight—flames twisting, white smoke on the wind.

She heard the noise then, as she had before—a high and far-off moan that sounded like an animal or bird or drinking human. Or was it the wind playing the mouth of an abandoned bottle in a ditch?

Now there was only the wind and the fire. She poked the trash with a stick and it collapsed in a spray of orange sparks. Something bad was going to happen. She knew that much.

Dan sat with the federal agents in the lobby of the Stone City airport, the official name of which is Barney Miale Field. Barney Miale was a barnstormer in the thirties and after the war he started a flight school that was in operation till the seventies. As a teacher he was said to have been impatient and even inconsiderate.

The agents' supervisor was stopping by on her way from Denver to Chicago. She wanted to wind up the Stone City investigation and Agents Anders and Lee thought it might help to have Dan on hand to show local interest.

"My bet is she shuts it down tonight," said Agent Anders. "It wouldn't hurt my feelings any. I'd be home by the weekend."

"Where do you live?"

"Vermillion. Me and my wife got a little horse farm up there and a Jack Russell named Patches, seventeen years old, can't hardly see anymore. Still works the horses, though. Gets by on smell alone for that."

"I got bit by a Jack Russell once," said Dan.

"Well, the whole breed is off its rocker, but faithful? My God."

The agent took out his billfold and flipped through photographs in clouded plastic sleeves.

"That's my wife. That's my nephew Bill. And here's old Patches. That's when he could see."

Louise washed and rinsed her hair in the kitchen sink. Gathering her hair on one side she wrung it out and gave it a shake, drops drumming stainless steel. She looked out the window. A red Mustang was parked in the driveway. She wrapped a towel around her hair and put her shirt on.

The doorbell rang, hollow from disuse. Louise and Dan rarely got visitors at night and no one rang the bell. She went to the living room and opened the front door a bit. A young man on the steps smoothed his hair and licked his lips as if his mouth was dry.

"My name is Jack Snow," he said. "I need to see Dan Norman."

"He's not home," said Louise. "If you have business, go to his office tomorrow in Stone City."

"What I have to say is better said at night."

"Oh yeah?" said Louise. "Might best keep it to yourself in that case."

"Are you Mrs. Norman?"

Louise gave a slight roll of her eyes. "*If you have business*—"

Jack Snow shouldered the door open and moved into the living room, jamming Louise into the corner by the stairs. The towel came loose and fell from her hair. She pushed the door gently, picked up the towel, and folded it.

"Whatever your problem is, Mr. Snow, you just made it ten times worse," she said.

"Call me Jack. Please." He strolled about the room like the arrogant house hunters of Louise's imagination. From the bureau by the front windows he picked up a ring that Dan had been given by the sheriffs' association, white gold with a blue stone.

"Put it down," said Louise.

"I'm just *looking*," he said. Then he sat down in an easy chair with his hands folded behind his head and smiled. He set the ring on the arm of the chair.

"So," he said. "Here's my problem. I lost my bookkeeper. I lost my partner. And my *understanding* is that Dan Norman drove her off. That's why we need to talk. Because without her, I don't know where the fuck anything is."

Louise held the towel to her chest and spoke calmly. "I'm telling you one time to get out."

"I have friends in Omaha."

"Yeah, well, congratulations."

Louise went to the kitchen, laid the towel on the table, and slid her stocking feet into snow boots. She grabbed a coat from the pegs on the wall, put it on, and zipped it up. Then she took a baseball bat from the broom closet and returned to the living room. Jack Snow was still relaxing in the chair.

"Hello, Red," he said. "Are you going to club me now?"

Louise headed for the door. "I'm going to beat on your car," she said.

She moved down the steps and into the yard. Jack Snow tackled her and she landed facedown in the snow with the bat beneath her. He rolled her over, sat astride her, and twisted the bat from her hands.

One part of Louise was scared, but the other part thought, Okay, he's out of the house. Jack Snow threw the bat toward the steps and pinned her head to the ground with his hand.

"This is what it comes to," he said.

He got up slowly, still holding her face. He edged away as one would from a wild animal. Louise did not move. He hurried toward his car. She sat up, scrubbed her face with snow.

"Go to hell," she said.

Jack Snow drove up to turn around by the barn. Louise stood and retrieved the bat. Her right wrist hurt but she could manage. She walked to the driveway and as the Mustang went past she swung the bat with both hands. Splinters of red flew up, suspended in the cold air.

Louise ran to the house, locked the door, and sat on the davenport. Her nose was bleeding and she tipped her head back and wiped the blood on the sleeve of her coat. Then she remembered Dan's ring. She slipped to the floor and crawled across the rug till she found it beneath the chair.

"Thank you, God," she said aloud.

She put the ring on her finger, went to the phone, and dialed Dan's number.

*   *   *

Jack drove to the warehouse. He knew his business was done and he felt he must have wanted it done. Leaving the car running, he got out to see the damage. The spoiler was folded and one end had come loose. He breathed the blue vapor of the exhaust gratefully and looked at the sky. The stars were out.

He jingled the keys from his pocket, but there was no need to unlock the bay door. Someone had pried it open. Not surprising, he thought. He pushed the door up and walked in. The relics had been rifled. Trinkets crunched and cracked underfoot. That was fine. He would get his money, drive through the night, be in another place when the sun came up. Start a life like others.

A light shone in the office windows, and he opened the door. A woman sat on the desk facing him. She wore a long purple coat, orange hat, and, around her neck, a silver torc from the inventory. He knew her at once, though it had been years since they'd seen each other.

"Sandy Zulma," he said. "Jesus Christ but I'm glad it's you. The night I've had, a familiar face . . ."

She leaned her long body toward him. "I want the rock," she said.

"What rock?" he said.

Sandra told him, as she had Louise and Dan, adding this time that it might be the stone of power that Red Hanrahan saw in the other world.

"Honest to God, I don't have a rock," said Jack. "Everything is on the tables. Or the floor. If you didn't find it, I don't have it."

"Of course you wouldn't leave it out for anyone to find," said Sandra. "You would hide it. I respect that. But now you must give it to me, or we fight."

"I'm leaving, Sandy. No fight. You win."

"Warriors don't run."

"I'm not a warrior. I'm a businessman. We were children. They were stories. Now we're grown, and we don't believe in such things."

"The stories are true," said Sandy. "You choose the weapon."

"Excuse me," said Jack, stepping to the desk. He opened a drawer and took out the revolver.

"Guns are for cowards," said Sandy. "That said, I will see what I can do with a gun."

"The thing is, I only have the one."

"We both need weapons. That's just common sense."

He raised the gun toward the ceiling and pulled the trigger. The pin clicked. He brought the gun down, swung the cylinder out: empty.

"Damn it," he said.

"You have swords," said Sandy.

Jack put the gun back in the desk. "Sandy," he said. "How can I put this so you will understand? Remember those daughters?"

"Which ones?"

"Oh, you know. They had one eye. I forget the name. Cúchulainn killed their dad."

"The children of Calatin."

"That's right. And the witchcraft they did. So Cúchulainn thought that clovers were soldiers and his land was being destroyed."

"Sorcery."

"That's right," said Jack. "And out he went, before his army could get together, and what happened? He died. You're like him. You're under a spell."

"Yes, but Cúchulainn would not have met his destiny otherwise," she said reasonably.

Jack took out the cash box, opened it, and stuffed the bills into the pocket of his coat. "I really do have to go."

She followed him from the office into the warehouse. He would carry on as if she were not there. Something hit him hard in the shoulder.

"Sandy, that hurt," he said.

He turned toward her. She had the point of a sword at his chest. And so, despite his misgivings, they took up swords and shields. In the old days they would have used sticks and the lids of garbage cans.

"You poor lost thing," said Jack.

The fight lasted perhaps fifteen minutes, though it seemed longer. They hacked and parried, charged and retreated. Sandy was better with the sword. Jack would use his shield as a blunt weapon to drive her back. Once he bashed her knee with the hilt of his sword, and she paced, limping, watching him with bright eyes. Jack was tired and bleeding from a cut on the leg. He wondered where they had found the energy when they were children.

With a cry of frustration he made a run at her. She slipped aside and struck his arm with her sword as he went past. Jack stood still. His arm no longer worked. He told it to lift his shield. It couldn't.

At the same moment, Sandy said, "The handle of my shield has broken."

Jack turned. The shield lay on the floor and the handle was in her hand. Her sword flashed in the warehouse light and landed above his collarbone. He dropped to his knees and fell onto his side.

Sandy put her sword down. She sat on her heels with long fingers resting on her knees. "Say the stories are true."

"The stories are true."

"Say you shouldn't have forgot me."

"I shouldn't have forgot you."

"Say you're sorry."

"I am sorry."

"You were my friend, Jackie."

Jack lost consciousness. A child again, he stood beneath a lilac and watched a girl walking down the sidewalk. She was new in town, arms gangling at her sides. Breathing the scent of lilacs, he sang a little song as if he hadn't noticed her and their eyes met and they smiled.

CHAPTER ELEVEN

THE HEADMASTER's instinct proved correct: Micah made a fine volleyball player. The game came easily to him. Playing, there was no past or future, just breath going in and out. The uniforms of the Deep Rock Lancers were black with red stripes down the side, a handsome, menacing combination. The shorts were long, the jerseys sleeveless. Micah liked riding the team bus and putting on knee pads and heating his legs with Tiger Balm.

The Lancers' coach believed that volleyball embodied many elements of life. The dig was survival, the bump was cooperation, and the set was prayer. The spike, he said, was going home.

He was unusually philosophical for a coach and in fact taught Introduction to Philosophy. Yet he hated to lose and would say things like, "Tonight I found out who has guts and who doesn't," leaving each player to wonder if he had guts or not.

The Lancers' record improved to 5 and 5 in the Conference of the Golden Sun. One night they played an away game against the conference champions, the Meteors of Mary Ellen Pleasant Country Day. Parents and students filled the bleachers, twiddling their phones, confident of another win.

The Meteors' gym was a vaulted palace compared with the Lancers' crackerbox. Rows of blue-white lights shone from the rafters. Nervous and disorganized at first, the Lancers fell behind. Micah took it upon himself to bring them back with a run of topspin serves that caromed backward from the Meteors' arms. Playing front court, he split the seams of the defense.

The Lancers won the first set, lost the second, and won the third, deciding the match. They danced in wide-eyed celebration, realizing the team they had become.

"Not in our house," said the Meteors. "Not in our house!"

"It's our house now," said Micah.

One winter's day, Micah and Charlotte went running along the concrete trough of the Ballona River. After a few miles they rested in a concrete underpass.

"Do you want to go to a show?" said Charlotte. "My mom got tickets from a magician she's dating."

"Sure."

"Or maybe you and Thea could go."

"Don't you want to?"

"Not if you and Thea have your hearts set on it."

"You and Thea have this weird thing."

"You are the weird thing that we have."

Then an old man, his face lined by the sun, came along pushing a grocery cart filled with cans and bottles. He stopped and looked at them, arms resting on the handle of the cart.

"I have beautiful handwriting," he said. "I use the Palmer Method. All the muscles of the shoulder and the arm must work together. Do you know it?"

Charlotte and Micah said they did not.

"Well, it's hardly surprising," he said. "The Palmer Method is a thing of the past. Only a few of us keep the memory alive. Watch now. I will show you and perhaps you will become interested and your generation will not forget the old ways."

He produced a newspaper and pencil from the pockets of his rain-coat, asked their names, and stood writing in quiet concentration.

"Done," he said. "Come see."

The capitals began with ornamental rings and flowed into looping letters. This is what the man had written:

Charlotte and Micah fix their gaze upon the youthful river.

He tore the page carefully and gave it to Charlotte, who folded it and put it in her hip pocket. Then he took up his cart and moved on.

Soon it began to rain. They could see big round drops splashing in the mossy stream. In the distance the handwriting man opened a red umbrella.

White light flashed around the underpass, followed by thunder, at which point the rain changed from light to heavy, falling straight and bouncing in fine spray from the concrete as the river began to move in rainbow swirls.

Seeing there would be no drier time soon, Micah and Charlotte walked into the rain. They were soon wet to the skin, locks of hair pasted to their temples.

After six months of living in California, this was the first real rain Micah'd seen. He and Charlotte raised their faces, laughing. There was nothing bad in hard rain once you accepted you were in it.

Micah drove Charlotte's pickup northeast through the city. He had no license, and was not old enough, but she had been giving him lessons in the empty lots of Mission Road. It was cold in the cab and she turned on the heater, which blasted old and rubbery air. Charlotte shivered and smiled with excitement.

The city looked like another place in the rain. The bright colors faded and you could see buildings as they were, old and patched with plaster and corrugated metal. Micah sometimes felt that if Tiny could build a large city he would build Los Angeles.

Charlotte lived high above North Main. A river flowed down her street, floating garbage bins of black and blue. Micah drove slowly up the hill, hardly able to see where he was going.

A neighborhood of small stucco houses gave way to open hilltops. Charlotte's house had three stories and was made of concrete with long terraces supported by wooden posts. It was unfinished and didn't look altogether safe.

Charlotte's mother was home in the living room trimming a fern that grew by the window, surrounded by a fringe of cuttings.

"You got caught in it," said Mrs. Mann.

"I thought you'd be working," said Charlotte.

"They canceled the flight because of a snowstorm in Chicago." She snipped a leaf from the fern and leaned back to survey her work and dropped the leaf on the floor.

"Because you see, everything in the flying world is interconnected," she said.

"This is Micah."

Mrs. Mann stood and gave him a pretty smile, much like Charlotte's only with tiny wrinkles around her lips.

"You need dry clothes," she said.

She went to another part of the house and came back with paint-spattered white coveralls in a neat soft square.

"These belonged to my husband," she said. "He was an artist and went to Big Sur to do his art, and that was the last we heard of him."

"Aw, Mom," said Charlotte, giving her a hug.

Micah waited in Charlotte's room as she showered. Horse trophies and ribbons lined the bookcase. He put the coveralls on the desk, picked up a journal, and leafed through it as gusts of rain battered the house.

Last night got falling down drunk which I know because I fell down. Had not had that much . . . or so I thought! 1 whiskey + 3 glasses of wine. But then I went outside for a cigarette and put it out on the ground and being thoughtful to the environment tried to pick it up. And that is when I fell over and hit my knee on a block of granite. It still hurts today. Know I should not smoke but sometimes I just do in spite of myself.

Feeling guilty, Micah closed the journal and put it back on the desk. Charlotte entered the room in a robe, the long black curls of her hair washed and shining.

Smiling bashfully, she opened the robe for a moment and closed it again and tied the belt.

"Now you know what that's all about," she said.

He blushed and looked away. She was eighteen and he wondered if three more years would make him so at ease. Doubtful.

Charlotte rummaged in a dresser, coming up with white socks and a T-shirt that she put on top of the coveralls for Micah to wear.

When the cuff of her robe rode up, he got a glimpse of red marks on her arm.

"Did you do that?" he said.

She pushed the sleeve up her arm and looked at the broken skin. "I should hope so."

"You've got to calibrate that bite, Char."

She pushed her hair behind her ears. "Yeah, kind of got away from me, that one."

Micah took a shower. Bottles of hair products lined the tiles and he looked at quite a few before finding one that was shampoo and said so in English. There were ciments and exfoliants and seaweed and other things that sounded like you would buy them in a garden store. Womanhood seemed highly complicated.

He dried off, got dressed, and went out into the house in stocking feet, happy as he'd ever been. Charlotte and her mother stood looking out the kitchen window at lawn chairs and tricycles and brightly colored toys sliding down the hill in the flood.

"People leave everything out," said Mrs. Mann.

She had made stew with meat and carrots and onions and ginger and small red potatoes. She dipped a ladle in and brought it up.

"Micah, tell me what this needs."

Micah put his hand on her hand and tasted the stew.

"It's perfect."

"It needs something."

Micah searched his mind for spices. He didn't want to get off on the wrong foot by recommending something ridiculous. "Salt," he said.

"I think you're right."

The three of them held hands around the table and Mrs. Mann said a prayer and they ate. The storm had made them hungry, and the sound of silverware in the rain was pleasant rather than tense. After supper they cleared the table and Charlotte washed the dishes and handed them to Micah to dry with a dishcloth. A small TV on the counter played scenes of flooded intersections, unmoored trees, snapping power lines.

"I'd better get home," said Micah.

Mrs. Mann was standing on a chair and moving things around in the pantry.

"I'm not going out in this, and I'm not sending Charlotte out in this," she said. "But look what I found."

Charlotte and Micah turned from the television. Mrs. Mann held a cardboard box with yellowed tape binding the split edges.

Charlotte groaned. "Not Risk. I hate Risk."

Her mother stepped down from the chair and brushed dust from the cover of the box.

"Charlotte loves Risk," she told Micah. "She's just trying to sound grown-up because you're here."

Micah called Joan. He spoke to her as Mrs. Mann gestured for the phone.

"Hi, Joan, do you believe this? . . . I know. I know. They're only guessing like all of us. I rather like it, to be honest. . . . So true. Anyway I have a couple of drowned kittens who turned up at my door, and they will be safe with me till morning."

Charlotte shook her head, hands covering her face. She dragged her fingers slowly down, showing crescents of red beneath her eyes.

"Drowned kittens," she whispered.

They played Risk on the floor by the woodstove in the living room. Mrs. Mann took Australia right away and captured Asia in stages. She would win, of course, as this is how anyone wins Risk. Micah based his pieces in Africa and Europe, and Charlotte kept raiding from the west, her mother from the east.

Mrs. Mann smoked a cigarette and tipped the ash on a plate on the carpet.

"It's always hard to win in Europe," she said sympathetically.

The night went on, wood falling in the stove and dice rolling softly. Around ten o'clock Charlotte's mother invaded Alaska with a force too large to dispel, and no one had the resources to take Asia or Ukraine from her.

Micah spent the night on the couch. Light flickered behind the stove grate and the house joints creaked in the wind and rain.

He slept restlessly. The shapes in the room were not the shapes he was used to. He dreamed of soldiers sitting around in a hangar. One played a harmonica. Ethan Frome came in from his school reading wearing a flier's scarf and asking if anyone had seen Mattie.

Micah woke in the dark with a hand on his mouth. Charlotte stood by the sofa in a white nightgown with roses on it.

"I can't sleep," she said.

Micah lifted the blankets for her to crawl under. He was still wearing the painter's coveralls.

"Can you take those off?" she said.

He stood and took the jumpsuit off. Underneath he wore only the T-shirt and socks she'd given him. Now he had seen what no one saw of her and she had seen the same of him.

They got under the blankets, face-to-face.

"I love you," said Micah, too fresh from dreams not to say what he meant.

She said, "Charlotte and Micah fix their gaze upon the youthful river."

                              *   *   *

A few days later, Micah was home in his room, still reading *Ethan Frome*. The characters could not catch a break. It was the fifth day of rain. They'd awoke to the sound of news helicopters over a house that might fall into the arroyo. The helicopters hovered most of the day before peeling off to the south when the house didn't fall.

Joan's husband knocked on the door. He came in with a box and sat down on the edge of the desk, hitching up the leg of his pants. There was something so adult about the gesture that it made Micah shudder.

"I've noticed something," said Rob. "In the mornings. You've been having trouble with your face."

Micah opened the box. It was an electric shaver. "Thank you," he said.

"It's the same model that Eamon has."

The shaver felt nice and heavy in his hand. "My dad would never get one of these."

"There are good arguments on both sides."

"Well, he saw this television show called *The Twilight Zone*."

"Oh Christ, Micah."

"Did you see it?"

"The shaver, the guy, the shaver comes alive, like a cobra, in the bathroom. . . ."

"So yeah, he saw that."

"'A Thing About Machines.' That's what it was called. There's nothing like *The Twilight Zone* in contemporary television."

"He's a different sort of person."

Joan and Rob attended a fund-raiser for film restoration at the New Gaslight Hotel in Hollywood. They were photographed in a step-and-repeat before a white backdrop with the restoration society's logo. A woman held paper signs identifying them, for surely, Joan thought, no one would know otherwise:

JOAN GOWER
FORENSIC MYSTIC

ROB HAMMERHILL
ANIMAL PARTY

Shutters snapped as a crowd of photographers yelled for their attention. They treated everyone like big stars.

"To your left, Joan."

"Right above, Joan."

"Don't smile, Rob."

"Down the middle, Joan."

"He's so demanding, isn't he?"

"Full front now. Full front please."

They went into the ballroom and found their table. After dinner there was a screening of clips from old movies before and after the film had been restored and enhanced.

An old man carried a birthday cake to his bedridden daughter six times with the colors becoming more natural with each repetition. Everyone clapped as if this were the most amazing thing ever.

Once Joan had shied away from show business gatherings, assuming she'd find herself out of place, but she had learned over time that, with the exception of caterers, most everyone felt out of place and couldn't wait to go outside and smoke.

After the program, Rob went to the checkroom to get their coats while Joan waited in the gold lobby. The green carpet was composed of sinuous vines and three-headed seed pods like eyes on stalks.

"Hello, Joan," said the screenwriter.

His face was red and his eyes looked larger and sadder than ever.

"Gray," said Joan. "I didn't know you were here."

"You're looking restored and enhanced this evening."

"You are kind," said Joan. "And you are drunk."

"I'm kind of drunk."

"My husband is getting our coats."

"I look forward to meeting him."

"Please don't."

"I saw you running one time," said Gray. "Your ponytail goes back and forth like a metronome. It seems so automatic it puzzled me. Shouldn't it be more random? And then I understood. It was obvious. Once it's back, there's nowhere for it to go but forth."

Joan turned away but he caught her hand and pulled her back.

"Or take lightning," he said. "It strikes the highest tree, we know that, but how does it know how high the trees are? It's not like lightning can see trees. The path is the answer, which must be formed from above and below."

"You're hurting my hand. This is getting weird and upsetting."

Rob came back with the coats. Joan considered introducing them as if everything was normal and decent, but then she realized with sudden clarity that she could just leave.

Under the awning, she put her coat on, buttoned it, and stood waiting. Rob and Gray were talking in the lobby. Of all the discreet people she might have laid, she thought.

Rob and Joan rode home in silence, listening to the rain on the roof, the splash of the tires, the unbearably tense sound of the turn signal.

"What have you done, Joan," said Rob. "What have you done."

She leaned her head against the window of the car. The glass was cool and refreshing. They drove by the Paradise Motel, where the lurid purple lights slid over rain-streaked windows. The only bond Joan could not break was with Micah. She was tired of all the other men in the world.

Chapter Twelve

Agent Betty Lee called Dan at his office in the morning to say they had raided Jack Snow's warehouse and found him dead.

Dan replied that the northern quarter of the trainyard was unincorporated so they should call the sheriff's office, for which he provided the telephone number.

Dan got coffee at the Red Robin and drove to the trainyard and gave a cup to each agent. They went to look at Jack Snow. He had cuts on both arms and a gash on the side of the neck. He'd died between a sword and a shield.

"Good God Almighty," said Dan.

"Maybe Omaha?" said Agent Anders.

"They would have taken the money."

"What money?"

"Look at his coat pocket."

"Oh yeah."

"He came to my house last night," said Dan. "When we were at the airport. Knocked Louise down. My wife. He thought I was the one after him."

"What'd you do?"

"Nothing. I wasn't going to leave after he'd been there once."

"You should've called the cops," said Agent Lee. "It might have saved his life."

"Or got some cops killed," said Dan.

They went to the doorway and looked out at a string of open boxcars rolling down the tracks. Panels of sunlight slid over the ground. They stood drinking coffee.

"Where's his car?" said Dan.

"That's a good question."

"I'd find that. At least there'd be someone to talk to."

"You say it's county jurisdiction," said Agent Anders.

"The city ends about an eighth of a mile over," said Dan. "Unless you guys want to claim it."

"Our instructions are to get out."

"What about that thing he was getting? That rock."

Then Dan remembered his conversation with Sandra Zulma at the Continental Hotel and thought maybe she was not so crazy as she seemed.

"It's not here," said Agent Lee.

"Anyway," said Anders, "the whole point of that was to get him to talk, which ain't happening now. This is local. This is homicide."

"You called the sheriff's office."

"They're on the way."

"They've got to come up from Morrisville," said Dan. "Ed Aiken is sheriff now. He used to deputy for me. Ed gets kind of flustered, but I bet he can find a red Mustang with a dent on the back."

"I don't remember a dent," said Agent Anders.

"Louise hit it with a softball bat."

"This is the Wild fucking West you got here."

"Well, she wasn't having somebody come into the house," said Dan. "Don't know how I'm going to tell her about this."

They heard a siren coming from the south.

The Mustang was at that moment parked behind the house of Sandra's cousin Terry. Sandra had come in the night when he was asleep.

She'd walked in the back door and washed the sword in the kitchen sink. Then she dried it off and treated it with 3 IN 1 from the cupboard and sat at the table working the oil into the blade with a cotton rag.

It was not much of a sword, but she would not likely run into somebody with a better one.

She scrubbed the sink with Comet and turned on the water, the blood and the scraps from Terry's plates running down the drain.

She yawned and took the sword into the living room, where she fell asleep on the davenport.

Terry made pancakes for breakfast, and they ate from china plates in the living room. He wore a blue sweatshirt with the hood up around his face.

"See you got some wheels."

"I'll be leaving shortly."

"Did you find Jack?"

"I did."

"What happened?"

"He's dead."

"He is not."

Sandra took the sword by the grip and stuck the point in the carpet.

"His chariot stands empty, Cousin."

Terry ate some pancakes and laid the fork on the plate.

"He is not. Sandy."

Sandra kept eating.

"It was fair combat," she said.

"I can't be part of this."

"I said I was leaving."

"I didn't see you. I didn't talk to you."

"You don't even know who I am."

Sandra Zulma wrapped some pancakes in aluminum foil and took them and the sword out to the car and drove down to the highway. She would never see Terry's house again. She'd not gone ten miles before a sheriff's car pulled out of a high and treeless intersection on Route 41 and fell in behind the Mustang.

* * *

Deputies Sheila Geer and Earl Kellogg followed the red car. Sheila and Earl did not trust each other, and Earl was not trusted generally, but they'd made an accommodation, part of which was that Sheila drove when they rode together. She'd been to racing school in Milwaukee and was the best driver of all the police in the county.

Earl could not deny her talent behind the wheel. In seminars he'd been forced to attend, he'd learned that women are as good as men in all ways, save upper-body strength, and that even this was an open question.

When they got close enough to the Mustang to see the bent spoiler, Sheila hit the siren and lightbar.

"Let's find out what she'll do," she said.

Sandra geared the Mustang back, the tach needle jumped, and the cruiser fell away in the mirror for a while before coming up fast.

Cresting a hill, she saw in the lane ahead a small gray pickup with a rust-stained refrigerator strapped upright in the bed. The pickup was meandering along and might as well have been backing up. The gap between the pickup and the Mustang closed at a sickening rate.

Sandra veered into the oncoming lane to pass and there encountered another truck, a serious one, a stone hauler with a high and dust-caked windshield and a mangled vertical grill like the teeth of a monster.

The drivers of these trucks are known throughout the county as the bat-out-of-hell drivers, for they brake for no one.

Nose to nose with the gravel truck, Sandra did the only thing she could, sliding the Mustang down into the ditch on the wrong side of the road.

The ditch was steep and flat at the bottom, and with amazement she found herself and the Mustang unbroken and hurtling down the frozen trough with the highway lost to sight.

She screamed then, full-throated, venting endless months of tension and boredom and alienation in the search for Jack Snow and the Lia Fáil. With tears streaming from eyes to ears, she felt her heart opening like a red-hot flower.

Then the Mustang hit the inclined berm of a dirt lane crossing the ditch and flew into the sky.

Sandra let off the gas. The engine sound died away. She couldn't hear anything at all. The car climbed above the land, and in the windshield she saw only blue.

She had hoped that the car would behave as flying cars do in movies—leveling off, landing, going on—but no, that's not what this car did. It maintained its upward attitude all the while, and, when it came down, the back end hit first, acting as a fulcrum with which to slam the rest of the car savagely into the bottom of the ditch.

The nose pierced the ice and the dirt beneath and the car flew again, end over end, chassis to the sky, coming down on its roof and sliding for quite some distance before bumping a culvert and turning slowly sideways in the ditch, smoking and ruined.

Dan Norman met Louise for lunch at the Lifetime Restaurant, where he hoped the fussing of the waitresses would give him time to figure how to tell her what happened to Jack Snow.

He took her coat from her shoulders and hung it on a hook and they slid into the booth and looked at laminated menus.

"We don't do this enough," said Louise.

"Hi, folks," said the waitress, a barbwire tattoo encircling her wrist. "Do you know what you want?"

"Go ahead, Dan," said Louise. "I'm still thinking."

"I'll have the BLT."

"Toast, babe?" said the waitress.

"Yeah. Wheat."

"What about you, angel?"

"Can I get the chowder?"

When the waitress had gone, Louise said, "She seems awfully fond of us."

"Listen," said Dan. "I have something to tell you. It's about the guy who came to the house last night."

"Did they arrest him?"

Dan shook his head. "He was murdered."

"He what?"

"Somebody stabbed him at his warehouse in Stone City. They don't know who. They're looking."

Louise began picking up crumbs from the table by pressing them with her index finger and brushing them off against her palm.

"I feel guilty," she said. "I didn't want him to die. Maybe for a minute I did."

"You have nothing to do with him dying."

"I was the last person he saw."

"There was at least one more."

"This is true," said Louise. "But, now, he's dead?"

"Yeah."

The waitress brought their food. She did not call them "baby" or "honey," "love" or "lamb." Maybe she sensed the bad news. They ate quietly. Louise said she didn't feel like she should be hungry but she was.

"Will the police want to talk to me?"

"I don't know. They might."

Leaving the restaurant, they ran into Britt, the chef whose mother had sold Louise the swing clock.

He unbuttoned his overcoat and unwrapped a red scarf from his throat. He asked about the clock and Louise told him it was in their bedroom.

"This is my restaurant," he said. "Come back at night. The dinner menu is better. Oh, and when you leave? I wouldn't go west. They've got the highway closed off for something."

* * *

Louise went east, Dan west. A cruiser blocked the road, and Earl
Kellogg was setting out a line of orange pylons. Dan rolled the
window down.

"It's the car," said Earl.

"Can you let me through?"

"Don't tell Ed I did."

Dan drove up and parked well back of the fire engines and cruisers and ambulances. The EMTs had cut the Mustang open and
were bringing Sandra Zulma up from the ditch on a gurney. When
they got her to the highway they let the wheels down and set the
gurney on the pavement.

Dan crossed the highway. Her eyes were open.

"I found him," she said.

There was blood on her face, in her hair, on her boots.

"Don't talk," said Dan.

They rolled the gurney away and lifted it into the back of the
ambulance and closed the doors.

Sheila Geer stood on the shoulder of the highway taking pictures
of the car.

"What happened?" said Dan.

She lowered the camera. "Love to tell you but Ed said we weren't
supposed to answer to you because you're not the sheriff."

"Well, Ed's right, really. I respect that. Seems a little defensive,
but his call."

"She damned near got herself killed is what happened. Missed a
head-on gravel truck by I am not kidding you Dan it couldn't have
been more than arm's length."

"You saw it?"

"Fuck yeah! We were right behind her. How this chick is alive
I don't know. She shouldn't be."

Dan walked down the highway with his hands in his pockets,
bending low to look at the crushed Mustang. Fire crews blasted
it with water. Few would have come out of that car talking, it was
true.

Ed Aiken struggled to climb out of the ditch with a piece of folded metal. Dan gave him a hand and pulled him up.

"I believe this is what we call the murder weapon," said Ed.

"Like as not."

"It has blood on it."

"Could be hers, I suppose."

"I realize that. Found this, too. Looks like we might have drugs involved."

He held a tightly wrapped cylinder of aluminum foil. Dan took it from him and tore the foil open at one end.

"Pancakes," he said.

The next morning Hans Cook stopped by Louise's mother's house as he usually did. Hans was Mary's gentleman friend of twenty-five years. He brought her newspaper in, made coffee, ran the curtains open for the light. And though it was cold he cracked a couple windows, for he would not have the place smelling like an old lady's house.

Mary was up and dressed in a blue corduroy smock, listening to a radio program of popular songs from forty or fifty years ago. The announcer had the unnaturally smooth voice of someone trying to soothe a dog.

"That was Susan Raye with L.A. International Airport, where the big jet engines do indeed roar. That is a busy, busy airport, one of the busiest in the nation if I'm not mistaken. Coming up we've got the Statler Brothers, checking in on the Class of '57."

"How do you listen to this?" said Hans.

"I like to have something on."

He turned the radio off and waved the newspaper in his hand.

"How about I read to you?"

"You do that."

He brought a dining chair in and sat beside her in the living room.

"Big headline today," he said, turning the front page for her to see. "Slay Suspect Nabbed, Getaway Car Flips, Sword and Driver in Custody."

"'Slay suspect?'"

"That's what they call them. Say, guess who's a contributing reporter. Albert Robeshaw."

"Claude's boy? He's mixed up in this?"

"He's just reporting on it."

"I listened to this on TV last night," said Mary. "A gruesome thing. Where were you?"

"Swimming."

"I find that hard to picture."

"At the Y in Morrisville. I used to swim a fair amount. Set a record one time for treading water."

"How long?"

"Oh, I forget. Five, six hours."

"Impressive. Well, go ahead."

And so Hans read her the story:

Sandra Catherine Zulma, 29, of Mayall, Minnesota, was apprehended yesterday after a high-speed pursuit that rerouted traffic on Highway 41 east of Romyla.

Police believe that Zulma was involved in the previous evening's killing of John Lief Snow, 30, who had been operating a Stone City antique dealership.

Federal agents investigating possible tax fraud raided Snow's establishment on the North Side yesterday morning only to find that the subject of their investigation had been slain in an altercation of unknown origin.

Local law enforcement officials were quickly instructed to be on the hunt for Snow's automobile, a late-model coupe that was missing from the grisly scene.

"Thanks to the fine police work of Deputies [Sheila] Geer and [Earl] Kellogg, the vehicle sought was located and stopped at 11:20 a.m.," said Sheriff Edward T. Aiken in a prepared statement.

And what a stop it was, according to Romyla resident Russ W. Roller, 41, who witnessed the spectacular apprehension.

"I was driving a refrigerator over to my grandparents' place in Lunenberg, because they want an extra one to put in the garage, why I don't know, when all of a sudden I hear a siren and see her [Zulma] coming up on [the rear end of my vehicle]," said Roller. "And I thought, 'Sorry lady, you'll just have to wait, because there's a [large] truck coming the other way.' But she give it a try. So things weren't looking too good for me at that time."

Police confirmed the essentials of Roller's account, adding that to avoid the oncoming truck Zulma took to the ditch, where her vehicle hit a rise and flipped twice. Freed from the wreckage by a rotary metal saw, Zulma was rushed via ambulance to Mercy Hospital in Stone City, where she is in fair condition.

No charges had been filed at press time, but requesting anonymity a member of the Sheriff's Department said a sword that may have been used in the killing was recovered from the wreckage of the Mustang.

Ironically, Zulma was interviewed last fall for this newspaper's "People in Towns" column. She said she had walked to the United States in a tunnel beneath the ocean. Due to the outlandishness of the claim and other issues, the interview was never published.

"The whole thing is outlandish," said Mary.

The back door opened. Louise called hello and they could hear her putting groceries in the refrigerator.

"It's getting to be Grand Central Station around here," said Mary.

Louise came in and sat. She took her hat off and held it in her hands and told them how, before he was killed, Jack Snow had come to the house looking for Dan.

"What'd I tell you about running around all hours?" said Mary.

"I was home washing my hair!"

"His mom was on TV, said him and the girl used to be thick as thieves."

"Poor word choice on her part," said Hans.

Mary sat back in her chair and closed her eyes.

"You always had the most beautiful hair," she told Louise, "but you would never let me brush it. 'I brush,' you would say. 'I brush.'"

"When was this?" said Hans.

"A couple weeks ago," said Louise.

On her third day at Mercy Hospital Sandra Zulma moved from the ICU to a room on the top floor, where Sheriff Ed Aiken went to see her in the evening.

He sat down on a chair by the bed and unfolded a piece of paper and read from it, saying that whatever she said would be used against her. She waved her hand.

"You have to say if you understand."

"I understand."

"Why did you come to Stone City?"

"To find a rock."

"That should've been easy."

She went on to explain the possible history of the rock, adding this time that it might also be the stone of invisibility the maiden gave to Peredur so he could fight the monster of the cave, or the rock slung by Cúchulainn to kill the squirrel on Maeve's shoulder.

"Did you know Jack Snow was here?"

"I heard he might be."

"From who?"

"People."

"People in Omaha?"

"I don't know where Omaha is."

"You thought Snow had the rock? Why did you think that?"

"A feeling."

"From where?"

"Inside me."

"What'd you want with it?"

"To take it home."

"You wanted to take a rock to Minnesota."

"No."

"Where then?"

"No place in this world."

"You see, now there's where you lose me," said Ed. "Did you kill Jack Snow?"

"Yes."

"And why did you?"

"We fought. His skills are not what they once were."

Ed Aiken left the room. Earl Kellogg was sitting arms crossed in a chair by the door.

"How'd that go?" said Earl.

"Pretty well, I think."

"Can I leave now?"

"Stay. I or Sheila will come spell you at midnight."

"At least go get me some magazines. If I sit here with nothing to do I'll go crazy."

"I know you told the paper about the sword."

"Prove it."

Sandra Zulma opened the door and peeked out of the room. The barrel chest of a sleeping lawman rose and fell with his chin resting upon it. He had a gun in a holster with a black strap over the grip. A magazine lay open on the floor. A woman in black lace had put him right out.

"Hey," she whispered. "You there."

Sandra stepped out, hearing the soft voices of the nurses at the station, and crept down the lavender hallway. On the walls were pictures of flowers, horses, mothers and children. It was that late-night hospital time when all is quiet and beautiful, and you can almost hear the sound of mending and dying. The hall was empty but for a doctor who stood tapping the chest piece of a stethoscope on the back of his hand.

"I'm walking," said Sandra.

"Let me listen to you."

He pressed the stethoscope to her chest.

"What is wrong with this thing?"

"Maybe I don't have a heartbeat."

The doctor touched her wrist with his fingers and looked at his watch.

"Adagio," he said. "That means okay."

At the end of the corridor Sandra took an elevator to the basement. The walls were steel with raised hash marks and she ran her hand over them, soothed by the cool repetition of bumps.

In the basement she found a long room lined with green lockers. There was a mirror on the wall and she looked at the bandages on her arms and face. Down the room she saw a young man wearing scrubs and hanging street clothes in a locker.

She picked up a mop and held it like a spear. "I'll lay you for your clothes," she said.

He looked at her, said nothing.

"That's all I've got to trade."

"You're off your ward. I know who you are."

"Got to have those clothes."

He glanced at a two-way radio on a wooden bench.

"Please don't do that," she said. "I don't want to hurt you but I will."

"Sometimes I don't get the padlock done right. So it looks locked but it isn't."

"You don't want to get laid," said Sandra.

"Not the state you're in."

"Maybe you could just hold me."

She let the mop fall and they embraced. At first he was afraid, but she held him tightly, courage flowing from her body into his. The man closed his locker, picked up his radio, and left the room.

Sandra dropped her gown and put on the pants and T-shirt and sweatshirt, the socks and boots, the watch cap and gloves of the doctor or orderly or whatever he was.

A door at the end of the hallway opened onto a ramp lined with dumpsters. Sandra stood looking up and down the street. A light soft snow fell, so little you could hardly tell.

A police car glided by with the ray of a fender-mounted light sweeping the sidewalk. She bent behind a dumpster with her arms across her chest and waited.

The Laughing Bandit struck again that night. Tiny sheared the padlock from the loading dock at Shipping Giant in Stone City. He liked using bolt cutters. There was something satisfying in the way the jaws bit and compressed before slicing.

Hard to pin down, the feeling he got using bolt cutters.

He took nine packages of various sizes and carried them out to the trunk of his car a few at a time. One had a yellow note taped on saying:

HOLD FOR AUTHORITIES
PER HERB

Tiny couldn't pass that one by. He left his trademark laugh written in blue marker on an erasable board.

Before setting out for home he smoked a cigarette in the car. He rolled his own lately, the tobacco reminding him in look and smell of pencil shavings he'd once emptied from school sharpeners. He liked making the cigarette rather than just taking it from a box. More of an earned smoke, you might say.

Through a haze of blue he saw the rangy woman walking down the alley, shoulders hunched and hands in pockets. Without a glance at him, she crossed steady from one side of the windshield to the other and kept on going west.

Bright ash fell from the cigarette to his chest and he slapped it out. He flipped the cigarette out the window, eased the car into motion, drove up beside the walking woman.

"Need a ride, miss? Where you going?"

"Minnesota," she said. "Couple hours from the Canadian border."

"I could take you that way."

She looked warily at Tiny, and she looked inside the car.

"Let's go," she said.

She walked around the front of the car and opened the door and folded her knees up in the passenger seat.

"I might not be the greatest company," she said. "I was in an accident. I'm talked out."

"I don't talk much either, not counting to myself."

It did Tiny good to drive roads he didn't know with another person. He had a pretty good idea who she was and wondered what she was doing out and about.

He stayed off the interstate for a hundred miles. Sandra dropped the seat back and fell to sleeping with the innocence of Micah.

In Mankato, Tiny stopped at a lonely mart and stood in the cold night, filling the tank. He wondered had she really done what they said, had she killed the man, or were the police bobbling along in their usual guesswork.

Inside the store he bought cherry pies and energy drinks.

"You have yourself a good night," said the clerk.

The roads were empty and dry in the early morning. Tiny played the radio low. The towns of Minnesota drifted up, islands of light existing for the time it took to drive through and then gone in the dark.

The towns seemed prosperous and orderly, but maybe it was only that he did not know them. The Minnesotans were asleep and dreaming in their beds. "Good morning," they'd say upon waking. "How are you this fine day?"

Steering with his forearm Tiny popped open another can of carbonated caffeine and drank it down.

Sandra woke when the sun came up. They were on the interstate headed northwest and making good time. Tiny was proud of this landscape, so far from where they'd started, as if he had built it for her. She rubbed her eyes, licked her lips, touched the bandage at her temple. When you awake is when the injuries hurt.

"Were you in the hospital?"

"Where are we?"

"On 94," said Tiny. "Coming up on Fergus Falls. There's a cherry pie there if you're hungry."

"Fergus," she said. "A great hero. He leveled the hills of Meath with his sword and needed seven women to get off."

"Now, who is this?"

She tore the paper open with her teeth and ate, the glazed crumbs falling to her lap.

"Yes, I was in the hospital."

"How'd you get out?"

"No hospital can hold me."

To pass the time, Sandra told Tiny the story of Deirdre, whose beauty had been foreseen along with the jealousy and trouble she would bring upon Ulster. Deirdre dashed herself against a stone post from a speeding chariot rather than remain captive to the killers of her lover. Or perhaps, as Lady Gregory had it, Deirdre drove a knife into her side and threw the knife into the sea.

"You don't have to make that choice," said Tiny.

"I hope I would be strong enough."

Two miles from the town of Mayall, Sandra asked Tiny to stop, for this is where she would get out. He would be glad to take her into town, but she didn't want to go there. He left her near a snowy path that wound its way into a state forest.

"Oh wait, almost forgot," he said.

He got out of the car, went to the back, and opened the trunk, where the boxes from Shipping Giant lay mixed up from the drive.

"I got these things."

"What are they?"

"Don't know. Stuff people sent. Take some."

She picked up two packages the size of shoe boxes and held one under each arm.

"I know you weren't coming all this way," she said. "You did this for me."

"Maybe I just like driving," said Tiny. "Open them."

She seemed weak and tired, and he unsealed the boxes on the trunk lid. A semi racketed by, and they stood still, buffeted in the backdraft. One of the boxes held a Boker knife with a hand-sewn sheath and the other a rock in bubble wrap.

Hell, thought Tiny, she would have to pick that fine knife. But she had made a good choice, which he could not begrudge. The rock, on the other hand, didn't seem worth the cost of shipping. Perhaps someone had intended to make a table lamp from it as is sometimes done.

Sandra held the rock in both hands, like something of value. Tall as she was, she seemed to grow and transform on the roadside, daylight coloring her face. She smiled for the first time he had seen.

"Do you know what you have done?" she said.

"Not as a rule," said Tiny. "That's a hellish good knife, by the way. Slip the sheath on your belt and you'll always know where it is."

Carrying the rock and the knife, she walked down the ditch to the path that entered the forest. Tiny watched until he couldn't see her in the trees. He wondered where she was going. Maybe a cabin. He put the empty boxes in the trunk. One had been the parcel held for authorities per Herb, whoever Herb was, but Tiny had not noticed if it was the rock or the knife.

He drove back to the house in Boris, arriving just after noon. He cooked a hamburger steak and ate some and put the plate on the floor for the goat to finish, which she did with pleasure.

Thus did Sandra Zulma escape what was called a dragnet but amounted to police of various affiliation cruising aimlessly and drinking the bitter coffee of the Stone City bus depot.

The Mustang lay flattened in the yard at Oberlin Salvage, collecting snow on the undercarriage, a cordon of yellow ribbon rattling in the wind.

CHAPTER THIRTEEN

THE RAINS ended and the sky cleared over Los Angeles, bringing the mountains closer. The family atomized as families will when a bad secret is hidden among them, a solid something they must all edge around.

Eamon worked on his senior thesis about Blaise Pascal, the French mathematician of the seventeenth century who invented the adding machine.

At first Eamon just liked the name "Blaise Pascal" but research turned up worthwhile facts, such as Pascal's terrible health and his argument for belief in God based on gambling theory.

Micah had started a school club called the New Luddites which opposed all things electronic. Made up of restless hackers and people who knew little about computers, it was never going to be a large club, having disavowed the means of communication by which it might have become known. "Live in the world" was the club slogan.

Joan and Rob went about the house like random people put together for some reason they could no longer remember. They argued over the making of the bed, the volume of the music, the foolishness of horror movies, Micah's continued shaving with a blade.

Every bitter word seemed to erode Joan's honor, because she could not be party to jealousy or unhappiness. It reminded her of the last days with Charles. She refused to discuss her unfaithfulness in the house because the children might hear. And when the children were not home she refused to discuss it because she didn't want to.

*   *   *

Rob had proposed to her at a ski lodge in Big Bear and that's where they went to decide whether they would go on or not. Probably they wouldn't, Joan thought. Once asked, the question had only one true answer.

At the lodge, large windows looked out at the mountains and trees and people riding T-bars in colorful and rising procession.

Joan had a massage and an herbal wrap in the spa, and they rolled her up in a blanket. She felt warm and relaxed on the table and thought she might lie just like this for a couple days.

Rob skied all day and came in burned from the sun. They dressed and ate supper in a restaurant with chairs made of tree branches.

Rob drank a glass of red wine and ordered another.

"Ski instructor walks into a bar and orders a round for him and his friends," he said. "'You don't have any friends,' says the bartender. 'That's okay,' says the ski instructor, 'I don't have any money.'"

"Rob."

"What."

"I don't feel like jokes."

"Oh. I'm sorry. Maybe we should ask everyone to be quiet forever."

"Be calm. Look at me. I am."

"Was it for the part?"

"I had the part."

"It's not a good part."

"I think I can make something of it."

"You fuck a ghost. This is drama. You fuck a ghost, you fuck the Screen Writers Guild, life is but a dream."

"It's not him."

"Why'd you do it?"

"I don't know."

"There is a process we go through, now, that is called divorce."

"Okay."

"You've been divorced."

"You know that I have," said Joan.

"You signed the papers."

"Yes."

"And where did they go? These papers that you signed."

"What *office*? How would I know?"

"Because there's no record of it."

"We're in a ski lodge. We're not in a court of law. Drop the show that you're making. No one is watching. You know I'm not good with paperwork. It's just you and me."

"This is over, Joanie."

"Yes. I think it is."

Later that night they sat on the veranda drinking wine under the warming bonnet of a heat lamp. Skiers went down the mountain under the lights, arms folded like wings. There was a yellow moon and Joan thought of all the things it had witnessed and would in time to come, and her own troubles seemed small considered in that light.

Micah and Charlotte went to the magic show at a theater on Beverly. You wouldn't have known it was a theater—blank sandstone wall, steel door, small placard on a tripod stand.

Doc and Dalton crouched on the sidewalk spinning quarters. The object was to stop the quarter on edge with your finger.

"Victory is mine, Little Man," said Dalton.

"That's on an angle."

"So what?"

"Doesn't count."

"I taught you this game."

"Get up off the ground," said Charlotte.

They went inside the theater and presented their tickets. It was a long space painted black with rows of chairs and a small bar selling wine and beer.

Doc and Dalton didn't want to be chosen from the audience, so Micah found an usher and told her his friends had pleurisy and could not participate in any magic.

She gave him red paper flowers of the kind distributed on Memorial Day and said if they wore the flowers the magician would know to skip them.

Doc and Dalton declined to wear the flowers as they would look like sissies, so Micah twisted the green paper stems together and, bowing, presented the two flowers to Charlotte.

"How thoughtful," she said.

The magician ate broken glass, made clothespins dance across the stage, and changed a traffic cone into a naked woman. He said that all the traffic cones in Los Angeles were people with a curse upon them and he was setting them free one by one.

Doc and Dalton were not called out of the audience and they seemed both relieved and disappointed. The magician asked Micah to stand during the mind-reading segment.

"I'm seeing a young woman," he said. "Her name is Lisa or perhaps Linda. She is far away from you."

"Lyris," said Micah. "My sister."

"Ah. Yes. And you're hiding from her. Why are you doing that?"

"Where are we?"

"You're outside. It must be a game of hide-and-seek."

"We did play that."

"And she's nervous. Why would that be? Even though she knows she'll find you."

"There were these cats that would come down from the old junkyard," said Micah.

"Wild cats. In the shadows. Yes."

"Big nasty calicos with burrs in their coats."

"What would you say?"

"To Lyris?"

"If she were here."

"That I miss her."

After the magic show they walked down to a private club past Rampart and beneath the freeway. They skirted a line of people dressed like mourners because Charlotte knew the bouncer, who waved them in, stamping the backs of their hands with red skulls.

They entered a sweaty tunnel of music that seemed to come from inside them. The walls whirled with lights, and dancers twisted and ground in a collective tremor. Micah thought of junior high dances where known couples and pairs of girls did most of the dancing, and to cross the gym from the boys' to the girls' side was to risk humiliation all around.

Micah and Dalton went to get drinks, then waded back through the room carrying plastic cups high in the humid air. Doc and Charlotte waited among walls of bodies. The four of them shielded the small space they faced, gulping the tops of their drinks before they could get jostled and spilled.

DJs stared like prison wardens from the mezzanine, shouting mouth to microphone, making sounds like someone beating a rug. They finished their drinks, and Doc and Dalton went for more as Charlotte and Micah danced. Micah was not that good of a dancer. Charlotte came to his aid with an unselfish ease learned over many nights in clubs. With their hands and bodies together Micah could not help but dance with some of her grace.

He became drunk in a little while and went outside and leaned against the wall of the club. He bummed a cigarette and smoked with his head hanging, until the ember burnt his hair, and then he put the cigarette out and went in again, raising the back of his hand like a symbol of solidarity with the bouncers.

There was trouble in the club. A man had felt Charlotte up and she had thrown her drink on him. He was in his twenties, which made it worse. The man tried to get to Charlotte, saying drunkenly that he only wanted to talk to her. Micah blocked him and they wrestled momentarily before the man hit Micah in the face and Micah shoved him back and lowered his head and rammed him in the chest, dropping him to the floor. On the black tiles the man struggled to breathe, and his eyes fluttered, and he passed out.

It was over in seconds and had gone just as Tiny had said it would. Then the sleeping man was roused by his friends, who picked him up and dragged him away.

Micah went to the bar and rested his elbows on shining bronze with faint cloudy arcs of the cleaning rag. His hands were shaking. No one knows what all we pretend.

He ordered water and ice and the barmaid took a plastic glass and thrust it in the ice bin and picked up a nozzle head and ran water over the ice and tucked in a slice of lime.

"On the house, Big Time," she said.

Micah went back to his friends but couldn't find them. He worked his way around the club. More people streamed in, faces assuming a religious aspect as they entered the music. Looking about, Micah saw only the sweat and sway of strangers.

He could not see all of the room at once. Maybe Charlotte was looking for him, and they were following each other around the perimeter at an unchanging distance, never to meet. He stood in one place for twenty minutes and then went out to find a taxi.

Micah thought that true cities would be full of taxis, but this was not the case with Los Angeles. He walked north on Glendale, looking over his shoulder, and soon gave up finding a ride. He had only a little bit of money anyway.

He passed a combination restaurant and meat market, a mesh fence topped with razor wire, a dark apartment complex with red slab roofs.

An orange cat lay on the steps of a canary store and Micah knelt and held out his hand. The cat's eyes gleamed gold from the shadows as it got up and wandered down to the sidewalk.

It arched its back in a big stretch and fell over and Micah scratched the fur behind its neck and under its chin. Cats loved this, in his experience, and this big tomcat was no different.

Micah sang a song that Tiny used to sing when he saw a cat.

"My name is Cat.
I'll pee in your hat."

Later on he met a man carrying a basket of laundry with a yellow jug of detergent high atop folded towels.

"Good evening," said the man.

"Good evening," said Micah. "Can you tell me if I'm close to Sunset Boulevard?"

"Just keep on, it's not very far. Go on up past Echo Park and bear left."

The 101 underpass was a dark tunnel with sloped banks of dirt and creeping ivy and the sound of cars passing overhead.

There were portraits painted on the columns holding up the freeway—a man making a fist to set off his biceps, a woman with hands pressed in prayer.

Micah came out of the tunnel into the electric light and walked along the western shore of the lake at Echo Park.

Palm trees bordered the water, lank and thorny against the sky, and three white jets of water rose, peaked, and fell from a fountain in the center of the lake.

Micah wondered if they performed a function or just made it look nice. Two helicopters drifted lazily in the charcoal sky.

He found a taxi at last in the parking lot of a Walgreens on Sunset. Two men, one large, one small, leaned against the glass-green fender with their arms folded and chins resting on their chests.

Micah got his billfold out and counted the bills remaining.

"I've got eleven dollars," he said. "Will that get me to Hellman Hills?"

They turned to each other with their arms still folded and talked it over.

"Not by the meter," said the smaller one. "Offhand I'm going to estimate that's a fifteen-, sixteen-dollar fare."

"Might be as much as twenty the way I'd go," said the other man.

He reached down and with both hands yanked a palm blade from the wheel well of the taxi. He ran his thumb along the leaf and tossed it aside.

"Well, that's all I have," said Micah.

"We run the meter, the meter doesn't run us."

They took him home, the small man driving and the large man riding along the high and moonlit curves of the freeway with the mountains rising in the north.

Micah sat in the middle of the backseat with his legs stretched comfortably, recounting the adventures of his night. The cab smelled of tobacco and oranges.

"You decked him out."

"It didn't seem like me doing it," said Micah. "It was more like I was watching it happen."

"Moments of action," said the large man, his arm flung amiably over the back of the seat. "Certainly. They pass by and later we . . . we . . ."

"Think about them," said the driver.

He laid his head to the side, relaxed, steering with one hand. "He got what he had coming. You don't put your hands on a woman you don't know."

"And even if you do," said the large man.

They laughed as if thinking of some woman they knew that they couldn't put their hands on.

"He got what he had coming," said the driver.

Micah had never been so happy to be in his narrow bed with the cool pillows and striped blanket. He fell asleep with the peace of the finally sheltered and did not wake until six in the morning when he heard tapping at the window.

He came out of a dream in which some of his friends from back home had moved into a house across the street. They ignored him at first, but then they opened up and discussed the crops they were planting.

Could it be raining? he wondered.

Micah got out of bed and wrapped the blanket around him and went to the window. Charlotte looked up from the grass, the white lines of the volleyball court rising behind her.

He went downstairs and opened the back door.

"Where did you go?" he said.

She reached out unsteadily, her fingers batting his lips.

"Shhh," she said. "It's very early in the sky."

"All right. You're hammered."

She looked to the side as if someone were standing behind her.

"No. I mean, maybe I am, that's beside the point," she said. "Hammered. I am hammered. You have the funniest way of talking, Micah Darling my darling. Come with me."

They went into the yard and stood in the grass looking at the sky, the midnight blue fading to yellow, the trees in black silhouette.

"Isn't it the most beautiful sky you've ever seen?" she said. "Why would they do this?"

Micah rearranged the blanket on his shoulders. "Who?"

"If you knew that, you would know everything," said Charlotte. She pressed her hands to her forehead and closed her eyes. "I'm sweaty right now. And dizzy. I believe I'm going to throw up if I'm not mistaken."

Micah took her hand and led her inside the house.

"Is Joan here?"

"They're at Big Bear."

"Take me to your bathroom."

Micah gathered Charlotte's hair and held it fast behind her head as she knelt throwing up what she'd drunk.

When the convulsions of her rib cage had turned to shivers, she reached up with her left hand and pulled the silver handle down.

She got to her feet and looked into the mirror on the medicine cabinet.

"I'm the baddest thing that ever came down the road," she said.

"You're the best bad thing I ever seen."

Micah ran water till it was hot and soaked a washcloth in the sink and washed her face slowly and tenderly as Lyris had done for him when he was young. She cried for a little while and then laughed.

Charlotte brushed her teeth and took a slug of Listerine and swished it around and spat it out.

"I feel like a fire has gone out in me," she said. "Can we go to bed now?"

They went to his bedroom, where he gave her a shirt to wear and she undressed, folded her clothes over the back of the chair, and pulled the shirt on over her head.

Her lean brown arms emerged from the white sleeves of the shirt one at a time and with her hands she smoothed the cloth down.

They got into bed. Micah sat and rolled the blanket out in the air and let it drift down over them. Charlotte turned on her side and patted her hip meaning snuggle up.

"Micah."

"Yeah."

"How did that magician know about your sister?"

"I don't know. I've been thinking about that myself."

"I love you."

Micah went back to sleep. Charlotte went to sleep for the first time all night.

CHAPTER FOURTEEN

ALBERT ROBESHAW drove up to Mayall to interview the parents of Sandra Zulma, wishing all the while they'd refused to see him. A reporter must question people bad things have happened to, but Albert was happier when they hung up the phone or closed the door, keeping their sadness private.

Clouds covered the sky, giving the streets of Mayall the look of old postcards from Louise's shop. The Zulmas lived in a Tudor house with a steep roof and an upright piano abandoned in a melting bank of snow on the curb. A melancholy detail, thought Albert. Perhaps Sandra had played the piano, and they couldn't have it in the house now that she'd gone missing and wanted for murder.

The parents met him at the door and let him into a cold and dark house. They went to the dining room and sat at a maple table with candles burning and red wax running down, as if Sandra were dead, which was possible.

The father was a thin man with gray hair on his forearms. The mother had short blond hair and looked sleepy. Albert turned on his tape recorder and asked about the piano but it turned out to be from the house next door. The neighbors always put things on their side, though they'd been asked not to.

"Where do you think she is?" said Albert.

"We don't know," said the mother. "That's why we're talking to you. To tell her 'Come home.'"

"She is our daughter always," said the father.

"They were friends," said Albert. "Jack and Sandra."

"When they were little I'd watch them out this window back here," said the mother. "Sandy'd sit cross-legged with her face to the sun and have Jackie scratch her back. She was always a very itchy girl."

"Some of them teased her," said the father. "She was smart and liked to talk. She was different. Kids sometimes aren't easy on girls. Girls sometimes aren't. Jackie was on her side."

"But something happened."

"They got older," said the mother. "Different things drew their attention. That was sad for Sandy. I know it was. I get tired of saying it. This was fifteen years ago."

"Is it fair to say that Sandy has some unrealistic ideas?" said Albert.

"Oh," said the father. "Certainly."

"From the books," said the mother. "We will show you the books."

"Did she go to college? Have jobs?"

"She was accepted at one college here and one in Maine," said the mother. "But she decided to take a year off, and then another year off, and you know how that goes. She did have jobs. She worked for the phone company. She worked for an organic farm raising string beans. Her last job she was a maid at a hotel in Lac Brillant."

"How did that go?"

"All right until she put some cars in the lake. They weren't her cars, she wasn't driving them. She just let off the parking brake and gave them a shove."

"Why?"

"No reason. What reason would there be."

"Did she ever have a run-in with the Boy Scouts?"

The mother yawned. "After the Lac Brillant situation, excuse me, she disappeared," she said. "She was living here with us again and we didn't know where she went. Honestly it was a relief. Isn't that a terrible thing to say? Don't put in that I said that."

"Okay."

"And the Boy Scouts found her," said the father. "Quite by accident. She'd been living in the woods south of town. In a den, I would almost call it."

"They've searched the woods," said Albert.

"Dogs, infrared scanners, state troopers. They never find anything."

"Do you believe she did what they say she did?"

The father folded his hands and turned his head aside. "What I believe is, she should come home."

They went then to see her room, down a hall past tall tables with faded linens, family pictures, dim lamps with shades of colored glass.

The gloom of the unused hallway was not unusual, Albert thought. Everyone sets out their possessions to portray a good and orderly life, and, when things go bad, the possessions become cold reminders of what might have been. That's what it was like. It gave him the shivers.

Sandra's room had drawings all over. A forest with winding path on one wall, a shadowy castle hallway with faraway hearth on the other, stars and quarter moon and darkness on the ceiling. And Albert wondered if she thought she had come from this place or was going to it.

"The doctors said drawing might help," said the mother. "I don't think they meant she should draw on her room but that's how she took it."

"She did it all freehand," said the father. "These are her pencils. These are her books."

The bolted metal bookcase leaned with the weight of a hundred books. They had cracked spines and yellowed pages. Some had grown thick from contact with water. Micah figured Sandy had left them in the rain or dropped them in the bathtub. They drew him closer to whoever she was, wherever she was. He began writing the names of the books:

The Táin
Mythology
Mythologies

Celtic Myths and Legends
Myths and Legends of the Celts
Oxford Dictionary of Celtic Mythology
The Mabinogion
Ethan Frome
Cuchulain of Muirthemne
The World of the Celts
Best of Mad Libs
Art of the Celts: 700 BC to AD 700
The Golden Compass
The Playboy of the Western World
Wuthering Heights
Beowulf
The Oxford Book of Death
That Was Then, This Is Now

Albert took *Cuchulain of Muirthemne* down and thumbed through the pages. With pink highlighter Sandra had marked a passage near the end: "I am Emer of the Fair Form; there is no more vengeance for me to find; I have no love for any man. It is sorrowful my stay is after the Hound."

While Albert looked at the books, the mother lay on her side on Sandra's bed, staring at the forest drawn on the wall.

"Do you have all that you need?" she said.

Meanwhile, Dan Norman drove over to the Robeshaws' home farm, looking for Claude, the father. A veteran of county politics and Democrat for life, Claude had been Dan's great ally when Dan was sheriff.

The Robeshaws were in the alleyway of the barn, ringing the noses of hogs to keep them from rooting up fences. They still kept outdoor hogs, did things the old way. Driving by you'd see the freshly painted A-houses in bright rows across the pasture. It was known that the family would never go the confinement route as long as Claude was alive.

Now he leaned his arms on a fence, watching two of his sons and his daughter-in-law at work. His eyes were barely open but he saw all that went on.

"We're getting on to being done," said Anna, wife of Nestor.

Oldest to youngest the Robeshaw kids were Rolfe, Julia, Nestor, Dean, Susan, and Albert, who had been the last to leave home. Rolfe, Julia, and Nestor had farms of their own.

"You left a message on my machine," said Dan. "Sounded like you were making a speech to the flower club."

"Ah, I hate those things," he said. "The sound goes off and I forget what I called to say. Which, I now do forget."

"About Sandra Zulma."

"Oh. Yes," said Claude. He took a glove off and examined the blue corded veins on the back of his hand. "What in hell's going on over there?"

"Talk to Ed, man. He's the sheriff."

"Here you've got a girl. Just out of a car wreck. Just out of ICU, for God's sake. Over six foot tall and no bigger around than a cane pole. And she walks away."

"I know it."

"How long have we had a Democratic sheriff?"

"Long time," said Dan.

The old man lifted his chin and pulled up the collar of his waxed coat and scowled, showing fine white dentures.

"We lose the sheriff, pretty soon we lose the board of supervisors," he said. "Next thing you know the whole place is run by maniacs."

"She'll turn up."

"How do you know?"

"Maybe she won't."

"I want you to think about running again."

"I have thought about it."

"Once you put the badge on, you never really take it off."

"You get that off TV?"

"Most likely. I heard you were up on 41 after she crashed that car."

"Yeah. Just happened to be going by. She told me she found him."

"I should say she did," said Claude. "You give it some consideration. Now come up to the house for dinner."

"Ah, I wouldn't want to bother you."

"I wouldn't have asked if you bothered me."

Dan and the Robeshaws walked up to the house, water welling in their bootprints. They washed up in the bathroom off the kitchen, as Dan had done thirty-five years ago when he was a teenager walking their bean fields with a corn knife. They still used the Lava soap that scraped your hands clean like stone.

The Moose in Stone City held a fish fry Friday nights, and Dan and Lynn Lord met for a working supper. Lynn emptied a worn leather satchel of folders and pushed them across the table.

"We have three new affairs. Suspected anyway. All you have to do is figure out which is which."

"This is the part of the job I hate."

"I know it, Dan. But they pay the rent. The economy goes up and down, jealousy is with us always. This is the season for affairs."

"Is it?"

"I've done the numbers."

"Probably has to do with weather."

"Ice. Rain. A kind of fatalism."

"What else?" said Dan.

"Shipping Giant got knocked over for nine packages. They'd like them back. It's that son of a bitch they call the Laughing Bandit."

The snow thawed in the daytime, and the water froze at night, making slicks that ran diagonally across the highways.

One night driving home from a tavern in Pringmar, Tiny felt the car drifting out from under him. He countersteered, and reaching dry pavement the wheels slammed into line with pleasantly predictable violence. He heard banging in the trunk.

He remembered the boxes he'd taken from Shipping Giant. When he got home he carried them into the house. There were seven left after the two he'd given the fugitive Sandra Zulma.

Tiny spread them on the floor of the living room, made a drink, and watched a TV show about paranormal investigators who visited places around the world troubled by aimless spirits. It was a poor show. They lugged a lot of gear, found next to nothing, and talked about the need for further analysis.

Still he watched it as he cut open the boxes. What he was doing seemed such a parody of loneliness that he had to laugh. He enjoyed being alive come what might.

Some of the items he had no use for. There were forklift binders and a woman's shirt, if that's what it was, all strings and straps and good luck to whoever tried to climb into it.

Then came a Sims game that Tiny would not play, but Micah used to have Sims. He would design big beautiful houses for them. The women turned fully pregnant overnight, and kitchen fires were common.

Tiny went to find the phone. It would be early in Los Angeles. He punched the number in and listened to it ring until a recording came on. Returning to the davenport he laid the phone on its back on the coffee table. The ghost hunters were snooping around in a dungeon.

"Would you like us to show you the way out?" said one.

"Yeah, that'd be great," said Tiny.

He opened what had been a nice food basket with wine and cheese and flowers, but he had to throw it all out because it had frozen repeatedly.

The last boxes held wind chimes, a necklace, and a dog collar with the name "Cody" etched in brass. Tiny went to the boot room and woke up the goat long enough to buckle the new collar on her.

"Now you are Cody," he said.

The phone rang. It was Micah.

"I got you something," said Tiny. "It's a computer game. Hold on."

He cradled the phone between shoulder and ear and picked up the box and put his reading glasses on.

"Sims 2: Bon Voyage," he said. "Looks like they're going on vacation."

"You got me a Sims game?"

"Why wouldn't I?"

"Doesn't seem like you."

"What do you think, I stole it?"

"Did you?"

"Yes."

"You're going to get in trouble."

"How are you?"

"I got a girlfriend, Dad."

The news made Tiny feel old. He sat down and moved the phone over to his good ear.

"A girlfriend, Micah."

"Her name is Charlotte. She rides horses."

"You open doors for her, all right? And don't let her get cold."

"Okay, Dad."

"They get cold easy. Or, you know, I'm sure they all don't, but a good many."

"I'll get her some gloves."

"There you go. And if there's a chill take your coat off and put it on her. That means a lot for some reason."

"I've got to go."

"All right, Micah. Love you."

He put the phone down, turned the TV off, and took the necklace out back to see it in moonlight. It was a thousand-dollar necklace. The links glowed silver blue in his hand.

A possum moved slowly along the tree line. The wind changed direction and the possum stood on its hind legs and opened its mouth wide, as if it had just said something hilarious and was waiting for the big laugh that would follow.

People who thought that nature was a happy playground should spend some time looking into the mouth of a possum.

Tiny retreated to the porch and sat in one of the church chairs rolling a smoke. The cigarette flared at the touch of the match and he held it upright like a candle till the flame died down.

Louise's mother and Hans Cook dozed in her living room, and Mary Montrose dreamed this dream:

Her old aunt from Council Bluffs had invited her to share an apartment in a tall building from the future. Long dead in reality, her aunt had been a masseuse in the fifties and wore red lipstick and pointed black glasses with rhinestone highlights.

Small airplanes of triangular design flew in and out over a bay. The atrium of the building went up to the sky. Mary's aunt lived on the twenty-fifth floor in a shabby apartment with spongy counters and soft appliances that would not hurt the falling elderly.

There was a hole in the middle of the kitchen floor, through which you could see the hole in the floor of the kitchen below, and so on, to the bottom of the building, if your eyes were good enough.

"I'm content where I am," Mary said.

"Well, they asked me to show you," said her aunt.

"Who did?"

"This guy from the leasing company. He's been after me—tell Mary, tell Mary. They have properties all over the world."

"Well, you told me, and I thank you, but I will be going now."

Leaving the building Mary saw a redhead reading a book in a cafe. She held the book in one hand and touched two fingers to her lips before turning the page. Mary knew her but could not remember why. And, when Louise looked up, she smiled agreeably, as if she too had forgotten that they were mother and daughter.

Dan and Louise slipped over to Grafton to make sure Mary had got to bed all right. Hans Cook met them in the kitchen.

"Louise," he said.

She ran to the living room.

Mary lay motionless in her chair beneath a green crochet, an arm resting on the side table. Her radio had fallen to the floor.

"Don't go," said Louise. "Don't leave me."

Dan took Mary's wrist as the radio droned *this feeling shared by so many of us, your host included, of being at a crossroads, of our lives, of our planet, it's no accident, it's very real. . . .*

Dan shook his head.

"Hans," said Louise.

"Yeah."

"Would you please shut the radio off."

Dan carried Mary to her bed. Louise turned on the orange lamp that had been on the dresser for years. She covered Mary with a blanket, knelt by the bed, and took her hand.

"You call the ambulance?" said Dan.

"They're coming from Margo."

"My mother," said Louise.

"She woke up. She'd seen you in her dream. Said you were very beautiful."

That was too much. Louise lowered her forehead to her mother's hand. Hans stepped out of the room. Dan put his hands on her shoulders.

Rollie Wilson and a younger EMT came from Margo in the ambulance. Dan went out to let them into the house. The red strobe of the emergency lights swept the front of the house.

"She all right?" said Rollie.

Dan shook his head.

Rollie whistled under his breath. "Mary Montrose. I'm not believing that."

"You go on in."

Dan stood in the yard looking around. The streetlights of Grafton shone on the abandoned feed warehouse across the street. The wind came up from the south, warmer than the air. The season was changing. "Mary Montrose is dead," he thought. It seemed as untrue as any sentence one could say. She had left town. He turned back to the house. It didn't seem right that it was still there. There was nowhere to go and nothing to say but goodbye. Mary had never liked Dan all that much except in comparison to Tiny. She had tolerated Dan. She was a little wary of everyone but Louise. Louise and Hans.

More than a hundred people came to the wake at Darnier Funeral Home in Morrisville. The room was gold and green and there were sandwiches to eat and coffee and whiskey and cranberry juice cocktail to drink. The children gathered in Sunday clothes on the stairway making sly observations about the older ones.

Louise sat with her sister June from Colorado and people were glad to see them together again and beautiful still, though it was another kind of beauty, having to do with light in the eyes, slant of shoulders, and the ease they felt with each other and their surroundings.

Tiny Darling wore a gray suit, tight in the shoulders and long at the cuffs. A tag hung from the back of the sleeve, and the old undertaker Emil Darnier appeared discreetly with small golden scissors to snip it off.

"I seen Mary over to Trinity Church last summer," Tiny told Louise. "There's this guy's going to make it apartments, but Mary said it wouldn't happen. She was just going by."

The sisters thanked him for coming, and he gave Louise a narrow black box tied with a ribbon and moved on.

Out of habit Dan had stationed himself where he could see the door, and Tiny crossed the funeral parlor to Dan standing by the cloakroom.

They had been rivals for Louise at one time and on opposite sides of the law at another and they'd hadn't said anything to each other in years.

"Glad you could make it," said Dan.

"Are you?"

"I just said so."

"Say I bought you a beer," said Tiny. "Would you drink it?"

"Why wouldn't I?"

"Some people got strange ideas."

Dan took a drink of Connemara. "If you want to argue go find someone who will."

"I'm only talking."

"How's your kids?"

"Micah moved to Los Angeles with his mom. Seems to be doing quite well by it. Lyris is around here somewhere, I believe."

"They're good kids."

"You know them pretty well, huh."

"Just what I hear."

"They are good kids. They're both smarter than I am, and that's how it should be."

Louise and June watched the conversation curiously from across the room.

"Didn't Tiny beat him up once?" said June.

"It was a no-decision," said Louise.

"What did he give you?"

"This." She placed the necklace in June's hand. Delicate silver links with a bar-and-ring clasp.

"Jesus," said June.

"I know."

Louise took the necklace and dropped it into her purse. "Not the place, not the time," she said.

Dan and Louise went through Grafton on their way home from Morrisville, as Louise worried she might not have locked Mary's house. They got out of the car and tried the front door, then the back door. Locked, locked. It was dark and cold. There was no reason to go in. Half a dozen deer tearing up grass in the backyard froze, then bolted, thumping haunches and vaulting hedges. There were deer everywhere in those days.

Chapter Fifteen

JOAN LAY on her back on the grass in the park, stage blood pumping from her breast, running hot and sticky down the grooves in her rib cage.

Her body twisted and she ripped handfuls of grass from the ground and then she lay still as the camera dollied around her on circular rails.

It was the last of Sister Mia. For the final episode of the season she had been gunned down by rogue police at a rally for immigration reform.

Rogue police made a useful plot element, because they implied that the rest of the police were all right. The camera held on the blades of grass in Joan's fist.

And cut.

And moving on . . .

Joan got up and stepped outside the camera circle and walked off bleeding in the sun. In her trailer she took off her clothes and the rig that pumped the blood. She took a shower and washed her hair and stood for a long time beneath the hot water holding her hair back with one hand.

She put on a soft white terry robe and sat drying her hair on a couch by the window. The hair drier sounded like wind in the desert, reminding her she was due to see her fortune-teller. Someone knocked on the door and she turned off the drier and called out that it was open.

Edward Leff, creator of *Forensic Mystic,* came in with flowers and Mia's rosary beads. He had discovered Joan in the St. Paul production of *Accidental Death of a Trapper,* in which she'd played a troubled game warden.

"You died beautifully," said Edward. "Thought you should have Mia's beads."

"I'm sorry it ended this way."

"A call had to be made, I made it."

"That is what you do."

"It won't please everyone."

"It doesn't please me."

"The people in the living room will wish it was me getting shot. To lose a character they love, it hurts. It's risky."

"She could recover."

"Wouldn't be true to the nature of violence."

"No. That would be stupid."

He put his hand on her shoulder.

"We began this show, Joan, you and me, at that bar in Minneapolis. I mean, *Mystic* was in the works, but so unformed."

"I remember. The Hilltop Tavern."

"Without you, there is no show. Without me, you're still in the boonies. What we did, we did together. What we did was good."

"Oh, be quiet."

There was a basket of fruit on the table and Edward picked up a pear and polished it on the sleeve of his jacket and took a bite.

"Just putting the emotion on the page."

Joan resumed the drying of her hair, and Edward left the trailer.

She hung the rosary beads from the mirror of her car and drove up to Shadowland to pick up Micah at school.

Everything was changing. It would be absurd for Mia to survive the shooting in the park. Moving on, and she would, as she always did. The sky opened wings of blue over the mountains.

* * *

Joan cooked spaghetti as Micah wrote a book report.

They'd moved into a new place following the breakup of Joan and Rob, their marriage nullified thanks to Joan's existing marriage with Charles, which made things simpler.

Now she and Micah lived in an apartment building on Rossmore with green gates and a fountain with the points of the compass etched on a bronze disk where the water fell.

Rossmore was a few streets west of Gower, which Joan told Micah was named for her. He knew better, of course. That was part of the joke. They had a furnished apartment on the seventeenth floor.

Micah wrote longhand in a three-ring binder. He stopped and looked up.

"This place smells funny."

Joan sniffed the air. "How so?"

"Like propane."

"No it doesn't, Micah. We just need to settle in."

"What if it explodes?"

"The apartment?"

"What if it does?"

"Micah. People have lived in this building for hundreds of years. Famous people, some of them, and not one of them exploded."

"Like who?"

The wall between the kitchen and the living room had a horizontal cutout that seemed to invite communication between rooms, but the top of the opening was so low that if you were in the kitchen you had to crouch in order to see more than the legs of someone in the dining room.

Joan rested her arms on the countertop and tilted her head playfully though necessarily.

"Have you heard of Milly Birdsong?"

"No."

"She was an ice skater. She won the Olympics I don't know how many times. Probably one of the best skaters there ever was. But you can't skate forever, so she came to Hollywood to be in the movies. Later on she broke her ankle on an escalator and ended up in radio instead. She played Hedda Gabler in a radio version of *Hedda Gabler*."

"Is that the most famous one?"

"I doubt it. I've only begun to learn the history of the building. People are a little slow to open up but that's only natural. I'm sure we'll learn lots of things we didn't know."

Joan put spaghetti and clam sauce on the table, and Micah set his work aside to have supper. Someone was playing the piano, and they could hear the music in the walls.

"*That's* a pretty song," said Joan.

Micah slouched with legs stretched under his desk in the back of the classroom. Miss Remora, teacher of American history, walked back and forth at the head of the room with a red rose in her hands.

The rose had no bearing on the lesson. Miss Remora just liked to keep her hands busy. She cried sometimes. She asked Micah a question about the Treaty of Guadalupe Hidalgo.

"Who disobeyed orders from the president to get the treaty signed?"

"I don't know."

"Did you do the reading?"

"Not all of it."

"Are you sick?"

"No, I'm fine, thanks."

Miss Remora wrote out a slip and sent Micah to see the headmaster. Micah wore a red sweatshirt and denim jacket and as he walked down the hallway he put the hood of the jacket up.

Mr. Lyons was soldering a circuit board. He taught shop class, in which the students were going to build kit radios.

"Now what do you want?"

"I didn't do the reading."

"Why not?"

"I fell asleep."

The headmaster dropped a bead of silver solder on the circuit board. "Are you tired now? Should I fetch a pillow and blanket?"

"Yeah, that would be nice."

"Put your hood down. I'm glad you stopped by. I understand you've started a club."

"The New Luddites."

"And this is what?"

"We don't like what computers are doing."

"Too bad for you, goat boy. Deep Rock Academy is going into the cloud."

"What does that mean?"

"In practical terms?"

"Any terms."

"I want that club killed."

"Can you do that?"

"Do you see the sign on my desk? What does it say?"

"You know what it says."

"Fuckin' A I can ban your screwy little club. It sends the wrong message to our corporate partners."

"But if it's what we believe . . ."

"Clubs are for medieval music and chess and harmless crap like that. What is it you don't like about computers anyway?"

This question pleased Micah, as it was the first of the day that he could answer.

"One, it's all about money. Two, the social stuff is a Trojan horse. Three, people do not see what is around them. Four, virtual talents are not talents. Five—"

"How many points are there?"

"Eleven," said Micah.

"I think I get it."

"I'm not going to disband the club."

The headmaster sighed. "We tell you to do the reading, you fall asleep. We tell you to fold the club, you won't."

"I play volleyball."

"That club is done. Get the word out. Do you understand?"

And with that the headmaster sent Micah to study hall to find out who disobeyed orders to get the Treaty of Guadalupe Hidalgo signed.

The decree to shut down the New Luddites came just as the club had scheduled its first action, in which the Luddites would commandeer the school's network and public-address system during fourth period. They liked using words like "action" and "commandeer." It would disrupt the school, if only for a while, and probably get them into trouble in the best of circumstances. And now this.

Micah called a meeting after school at the stone wall down the hill where they could not be overheard. The Luddites assembled— Cilla, Rafa, Dakota, Micah, and Silas—joined by Eamon with his black guitar case.

"Rafa will update us on the action," said Micah.

"We're through the firewall," said Rafa. "Ran two tests from home the other night. Put up a photograph of Emily Browning and played some Mozart for precisely ninety seconds. The network resumed without incident."

"How do you know?"

"I'm tight with John the janitor. I give him weed from time to time. He confirmed from the teachers' lounge."

"Excellent," said Micah. "Eamon. Where are we with music?"

"It's been a while since we talked about this," said Eamon, and Micah got his meaning—they'd been living in the same house when the plan was first considered. "I didn't want anything too obvious. So my recommendation is 'Fake Empire' by the National."

"And could you play that for us now?"

Eamon opened the guitar case and took up his Gibson Archtop with loving care, tuned it, and played and sang the song while sitting on the grass.

A trance came over the Luddites as they listened to the song of staying out late and picking apples and dancing on ice and being half-awake in the empire of the title.

"Show of hands," said Micah, and all hands raised as one. There were tears in Cilla's eyes.

"I've got the title card," she said softly. From her backpack she brought a big black placard with white letters in the unforced free-hand that comes so naturally to girls:

LIVE IN THE WORLD
THE NEW LUDDITES

"We might want to change the words," said Micah. "Lyons told me yesterday to shut down the club. It conflicts with our corporate masters."

"Oh, no," said the Luddites, "You've got to be kidding," and the like. Eamon chewed a licorice whip like field straw and glanced around as if considering more interesting places he could be.

"Why are we even talking about the action?" said Dakota. "If we're not a club anymore."

"Lyons told me to get the word out," said Micah, looking at each of them in turn. "So that's what we're going to do."

"He'll kill us," said Silas. "Throw us off the towers one by one. Birds will eat our bones."

"This could go on our transcripts," said Dakota.

Micah had poor grades and seemed as likely to be back home in Boris or living under a bridge as going to college in four years, so transcripts did not enter into his thinking.

"It will be our first and last action," he said. "I'm in it till the end. Anyone who wants to withdraw, I think we'll understand. Eamon, you're a senior. What do you advise?"

Eamon closed his guitar case. "Do it."

"Just get me the visual," said Rafa. "I'll find an MP3 of 'Fake Empire.'"

Micah caught up to Eamon as he walked to the parking lot. "Are you mad at me?"

"I'm not mad at you," said Eamon, repeating the words as people do when they're mad at you. "I don't know what to think."

"Did your dad tell you what happened?"

"What did?"

"We don't talk about it. I don't want to know."

"I think she was seeing somebody."

Micah nodded and rubbed his eyes. "You know what? Joan has left both our fathers."

"I never thought of that," said Eamon. "I kind of miss her. The way she smiled. She floats along in her world. You can't tell what she's thinking. Maybe she isn't thinking anything."

"You should come to the apartment. She'd love to see you."

"What's it like?"

"Small. She sleeps in the living room and I sleep in the bedroom. There's a trash chute in the hallway. You open the door and throw the stuff in and it falls forever. You don't even hear it land sometimes."

"Sounds nice. It was okay, being your brother."

"You still are if you want to be," said Micah.

The action took place the following Tuesday. For three minutes and twenty-seven seconds, the National's recording of "Fake Empire" played and computer programs shut down, replaced by the message:

The New Luddites have been disbanded by order of the Headmaster. Let no one disband an idea. Live in the world.

The song began with a lone organ note that gave way to four rolling chords of bass and piano and then the singer's voice, deep and glassy. *Tiptoe through our shiny cities, with our diamond slippers on.* The music came from all over the school. Teachers paused, chalk stilled in their hands, gazing at the ceiling. Kids rose from their desks and drifted to the hallways as if looking for the band. *Let's not tyry to figure out everything at once.* People danced elegantly at first and then wildly when the manic horn section began. Mr. Lyons emerged from the administration offices and paced with folded arms until the end of the song.

"Where is Micah Darling?" he said.

Micah pushed through the crowd. "Present, Headmaster."

"This is my school."

"Well, I don't agree with that," said Micah. "The school belongs to all of us."

There was quiet. Everyone seemed to be considering whom the school belonged to. It was not a simple question. Without Mr. Lyons there would still be a school, but wihtout the students, what would there be? People in offices with nothing to do. Then the silence broke into cheering and clapping and whistling and requests for the song to play again.

"Go to your homerooms," said Mr. Lyons. "The next one who makes a sound will be suspended. The Luddites are suspended. Darling, you're expelled. Your parents shall be notified."

"Our address has changed," said Micah.

There were three weeks left in the school year. Micah spent them at the beach. He would take the bus down to Crenshaw and Venice and another bus west.

Joan gave her blessing. They couldn't afford the school, and she thought that Micah had been mistreated for an event that showed initiative and creativity.

If all the midways of all the fairs he'd ever seen were pushed to the edge of the continent, Micah thought, they would make a place like Venice Beach.

Music played and dogs barked, skateboards clacked and seagulls pierced the ocean air with their greedy calls. Lots of birds were hungry but few had the seagull's sense of owning all things that could be eaten. Refugee rows of shops sold henna tattoos and massages, shark teeth and Tarot readings, your name on a grain of sand.

Many parts of Los Angeles had next to no pedestrians, and that might have been because they were all here and dressed like

professional athletes on their day off. Along the waterfront prom-
enade they traveled on foot and skates, on rented bicycles and Segway scooters that had caught on here if nowhere else.

One man on a Segway rode about pointing things out to himself
and commenting into a tape recorder. A Segway family glided along,
the children on smaller models.

Painted on the wall of a hostel and watching it all was the Venus
of Venice Beach, who wore blue leggings and a pink camisole and
thought that history was myth.

Micah played volleyball on the sand beside the flat white ocean.
He didn't play hard in these games. He'd smoke a serve or smother
a spike sometimes, but in the spirit of the beach he was not looking
to show anyone up.

Late one day he walked along the row of shops. A man skated
in and out of the crowd with an electric guitar, a body-mounted
amp, and a bandolier of batteries. He plucked complex chords that
lingered as he glided by.

"Fly on, Little Wing," said a lady in a straw hat.

Micah walked into a medical marijuana shop, a clean and orderly
space with canvas awning. It was like a candy store, with backlit
cabinets and glass counters offering weed in plastic bags and glass
jars with silver lids.

"And how are we today?" said a man in a white coat with pens
in the pocket.

"Very well, thank you," said Micah. "I'd like to get certified."

"How old are you?"

"Fifteen."

"You have to be eighteen or accompanied by a parent or guardian.
Can you bring your mother or father in?"

"No."

"What's the problem?"

"They just wouldn't."

"I mean the medical problem."

"Ringing in the ears."

"Come back when you are older and have a California ID. Will you do that?"

"Oh, probably not," said Micah.

He left the shop and ate a hot dog on a bench facing the ocean. He felt a profound and enjoyable emptiness.

Soon a man in his twenties came along and sat beside him. He had a red beard and sunglasses and worn leather sandals.

"I saw you at the marijuana doc's," he said.

"You have to be eighteen."

The man took a silver cigarette case from his pocket and gave Micah a joint.

"Look eighteen to me."

"Thank you."

The man's name was Mark. He'd come down from Olympia after graduating from college. His father was a software maker who'd helped him get a little house and a shop that sold shirts and jewelry.

"I've seen you playing volleyball."

"Yeah, I like it."

Micah got high, his thoughts fading to simple awareness of the ocean. He felt made of stone. If seagulls attacked he would probably just sit there getting pecked.

You never knew what you were getting with weed. Probably someday it would all be as uniform as alcohol. The sun bled red into the water and the ringing in his ears fell to a whisper.

"I like volleyball," he said.

"You want to get in a real game, I know some people. They play at night on other beaches. Gets pretty serious."

"Where would you end up if you just started swimming?" said Micah.

"Channel Islands."

"How far is that?"

"Twenty miles."

"And then what?"

"Japan."

"How far is that?"

"Way out there."

"I want to go to Japan."

"Fuck, man," said Mark. "Fly out LAX tonight you got the money."

"I don't have the money."

"Japan is beautiful."

"Have you been there?"

"No."

Mark invited Micah to have supper with him and his girlfriend. They lived in a narrow yellow house with flowers and vines on a street going down to the ocean.

You could see far into the house from the street. The furniture was white and orange and green, and there were paper lanterns.

Mark's girlfriend, Beth, had green eyes, freckles, and strawberry-blond hair parted on the side. She didn't mind that her boyfriend had brought home a stray from the beach. Maybe people were like that here.

Micah called Joan to say he was having supper with friends. Now that they were living in the apartment, she had a better sense of when he was home and when he wasn't.

They had vegetarian curry, soft bread called naan in a woven basket, red wine in two-dollar bottles from Trader Joe's.

Beth came from St. Louis. She was a nurse and the daughter of a minister who was very strict and she was glad to be away from his world.

She worked at a clinic in Lomita and painted in her spare time. She liked to paint little bits of ocean as seen through cars or people's legs or over rooftops.

After supper they sat in the living room, and Micah explained how he got expelled from school. They thought it was a wonderful story, though, as Micah told it, he saw that it was a silly thing that didn't amount to much and wouldn't make the school right.

Micah stayed the night on Mark and Beth's couch. He could not sleep and went to the kitchen sink and drank glass after glass of water. A friendly light shone from beneath the cupboards.

He went back to the front room and lay down beneath a quilt. An hour later he heard the refrigerator open, and then Beth came into the front room with a bottle of grapefruit juice.

"Sleeping?" she said.

"Not yet."

She placed pills in his hand.

"What is it?"

"Painkiller."

"It helps you sleep?"

"It passes the time till you do."

Micah looked at her, and she said, "I'm a nurse, baby. First I do no harm."

They took the pills and washed them down with the grapefruit juice and went out to sit on the front porch by the street.

It was a clear night. The moon rode high above the blue roofs of the beach town. Micah felt no restlessness, no sorrow. There was a soft and intermittent breeze.

After a while skateboarders came rolling down the street. They leaned back looking around with long hair and cool blank expressions.

"There they go," said Micah. "Down to the sea."

Chapter Sixteen

THE TRAIL of the Laughing Bandit took Dan Norman to Aqualung Spas of Stone City. He stood with the owner in the showroom, by a hot tub bordered in cedar planks.

"Are we a target?" said the owner, a former minor league slugger with a big yet solid gut. Once played for Duluth in the Northern League.

"You fit the profile," said Dan. "You're on the highway. Got a loading dock in back."

"Spa parts ain't much use 'less you have a spa."

"The guy's a pack rat. No pattern in what he takes. Now, what I'd like to do is give you a box. There's a couple wrenches inside for weight and a beacon. You set it out at night, take it in come morning. See if he won't swipe it, and we find out where it ends up."

"Other places doing this?"

"Big Wonder is. World of Wheels is."

"It's in everybody's interest."

"That's what I'm hearing."

"You and Louise have a spa?"

"We don't."

"Well, I wouldn't go all salesman on you."

"I appreciate that."

"Do you good, though. Most of us are raised to think of comfort and relaxation as bad somehow."

"I expect there is some of that."

"Some. I'm here to tell you it is rampant."

He turned the hot tub on. The engine hummed, the water churned, the floor vibrated. It seemed like a lot of commotion for a bath.

"It's hydrotherapy," said the owner. "Return to the sea with your loved one. We work hard. I know you must. The world is cold. Are we not entitled to comfort? Even pleasure. And yes I will use that word. All for pennies a day."

"You are going all salesman on me."

"Can't help myself. I believe in spas."

"I can see that you do."

People thought Louise would be lost without Mary, and there was something to that. So much of herself had been formed in response to Mary's judgments that now she didn't seem to be formed of anything.

She put up a sign in the thrift shop window saying CLOSED UNTIL FURTHER NOTICE. The metal shutters came down over the stuffed crow, which looked away as if abandoned by its protector. Then she took the Scout to Ronnie Lapoint's shop in Morrisville.

"What's this thing doing to you now, Louise?"

"Pulling to the left."

"Uh-huh."

"I was hoping you could fix it."

"No way I can do it now. For you though I will."

"You're the best."

Louise read *Scientific American* in a waiting room smelling of Glade and grease and gasoline. The television played without sound a talk show featuring three women who seemed so engrossed in their topic that they might jump up and dance.

Ronnie came in after a while, wiping his hands on a red flannel rag.

"Sure sorry about your mom."

"Oh. Thanks, Ronnie."

"I want to say my condolences, but what are condolences?"

"I think you just gave them."

"That lady could argue me up one wall and down the other."

"That's my mom. How's the truck?"

"You won't have the pulling. But she really needs rings."

"How much are rings?"

"Aw, it's not worth putting rings in."

Louise drove to North Cemetery on a hill outside Grafton. Robins walked about with long strides in the uncut grass. She put flowers down on Mary's grave, a hill of dirt covered in green fabric. She waited for revelation. Mary had done her part to make her world go around, and it had gone around seventy-seven summers—not so many when you thought about it, her life ending in a dream, and she never spent one day in a nursing home. Louise rolled up the green cloth and left it by the maintenance shed, because Mary would prefer the honest dirt.

Louise went to her baby's stone, which always needed tending in the spring, as it was flush with the ground, and grass tended to grow over it. She trimmed the grass and troweled away the dirt and scrubbed the gray slate with rags. MAY 7, 1992.

"I wish you were here," she said.

From the cemetery she went to see Don Gary and Lyris about a headstone.

The fragrant and industrious Don Gary told of a ballgame he'd seen once at the Metrodome. The clean-up hitter was on deck, and Don looked forward to seeing him hit a home run or strike out or whatever he would do. The score was tied, men on base, tense. It was a long story and to Don's thinking a parable about losing a parent. Louise stopped paying attention to the words, but she liked the sound of him talking.

A manila envelope addressed in red ink landed on the desk of Albert Robeshaw at the newspaper in Stone City.

The office was built before the print business went into decline, and before the old editor making good money had been fired in favor of a new editor making poor money. Probably it would cost more to take the office apart than to leave it.

Albert sat at a table by the vending machines and opened the envelope, which contained a letter and a map sent by a man who lived in Mayall, Minnesota.

Dear Mr. Robeshaw,
I have followed with interest your coverage of the missing Sandra Zulma, however I wish to clarify a statement in the recent article "Fantasy Life of a Fugitive." The encounter between Sandra Zulma and the Boy Scouts took place in the State Forest not the Fen, where overnights are not permitted because of the native plants. See map (enclosed). This is a minor imperfection in an outstanding article, sir. I was one of the scouts who discovered Sandra Zulma on the river. You can be sure I remember that day.

Albert spread the map on the table. It showed the state forest and a winding river with an X drawn on either side, one labeled *Scout Encampment* and the other *Sandra Zulma*.

Albert wondered whether the newspaper would need to print a correction. The new editor kept track, so one didn't correct lightly.

He took the correspondence to the city editor, who had been with the paper for years and made more money than anyone else. She was hoping to get bought out rather than fired.

"Hey, what do you make of this?" said Albert.

She took the letter from Albert and looked at the dense handwriting.

"I'm not about to read this," she said.

Albert took the letter back and paraphrased it.

"Did we say it was in this fen thing?"

"We said in the woods."

"And that's accurate."

"Yeah."

"Fuck it. Inside baseball."

"That's what I thought. Maybe I should go up there."

"No you shouldn't. Our out-of-town money is spent, and you spent it. Now listen, honey. I want you to slip over to the American Suites. There's a greenhouse conference going on."

"A greenhouse conference."

"Yeah. You know, with plants. See what they're talking about. If there's some new hybrid. Have fun with it. People love greenhouses."

Dan Norman wandered the Great Hall of the American Suites, where the spring meeting of the Garden Supply Consortium of the Upper Midwest was taking place.

He was monitoring two unrelated cases of suspected infidelity. That was four people counting the partners. Apparently these greenhouse operators were highly sexualized, perhaps from being around seeds and earth and growing all the time.

The private investigation business relied on this simple work, but Dan felt like a crumb. Whatever you found out, you seemed to be taking financial advantage of the death of a marriage.

To which Lynn Lord would say, "Well, far as that goes, Dan, if you're too sensitive to take financial advantage of things, you shouldn't be in any business. You should go be a monk, get yourself one of them monk haircuts."

Moving with the tide of conventioneers, Dan strolled booth to booth, holding the Fanta camera that had nailed the clandestine bowler. He checked out the latest in spray nozzle technology.

Every couple years he or Louise would buy one of these, but it would always break or disappear, and they would go back to thumbing the end of the hose to wash the car or chase leaves down the eaves trough.

Dan paused at a booth crowded with concrete statues—trolls and mermaids, deers and frogs and eagles, naked people who seemed to be stretching after a restful nap and wondering where they put their clothes.

The nipples of the female statues were concealed by strategically placed arms or vines or locks of hair, and the men all had very small penises, but then, when you thought about it, there probably wouldn't be that much of a market for a garden statue with a large penis either.

The statues reminded Dan of the adulterers. He had not seen any of them for a while. Possibly they were in their rooms, under the covers. He left the Great Hall, and in the corridor he saw one of the couples.

They didn't seem quite old enough to be married to other people they'd got tired of. The man had his back to the wall, and the woman leaned close holding his face in both hands.

Dan could not ask for a better chance to get them on video. As they were standing by the elevators, he could move naturally down the hall with his attention trained on them the whole time.

All he had to do was turn the camera on and walk over and take the elevator to any floor. He put his finger on the button that would turn the camera on, and, as he did so, he asked himself why should he do this, and saw that there was not one reason in the world.

He turned and walked to the hotel lobby, where Albert Robeshaw was just coming in.

"Hey, Dan," said Albert. "I'm looking for the greenhouse convention."

"Just go on down that hall."

"What are you doing?"

"Working."

"What on?"

"Ah, it doesn't matter. I quit."

"The whole thing."

"Yeah."

"What will you do?"

"Not sure. Your dad's after me to run for sheriff again."

"You would win."

"I might. And if I don't maybe I'll just be a monk or something."

"You'd be a great monk."

"You think so?"

"Well. A good one, anyway."

Dan drove home, coming up on Delia Kessler's place. She and Ron were divorced now, and the kids had long since moved away. LABS FOR SALE, said a sign.

Dan parked in the lane. The house was a prefab that had been brought in after the spectacular Kessler fire of the nineties. It was long and gray with small windows and looked like an ocean liner.

Dan knocked on the side door and Delia let him into the kitchen, where she was cooking something in a speckled black pot.

"What're you making?"

"Oyster stew."

"I seen your sign. You've got pups."

"Too late," said Delia. "They've all gone but for one, and her I'll probably keep."

"To breed," said Dan.

"Nah. I think she's a little slow. The last one to go, they're never happy about it, but she hasn't come around the way they do. I charge a fair price, and I don't want it out there I'm selling depressed dogs. I mean I'll show her to you but don't expect too much."

"Might as well have a look."

Delia put a wooden spoon on a porcelain rest, turned the fire down, and led the way to the room where she kept the litters.

The dog room smelled like pee. There was a wire crate with blankets inside and brittle newspapers spread on the floor. "Sword Killer Escapes in Daring Hospital Break," said an old headline.

The Lab pup lay underneath a water heater, eyes brown and slightly crossed.

Dan knelt on the newspapers, and the dog yawned, stuck her head out, and smelled his hand.

Delia stood in the doorway, chewing the skin by the nail of her little finger.

"She's certified hips and eyes. Just kind of withdrawn."

"How much?"

"Three hundred."

The dog cocked her head, as if the price sounded high and she wondered if Dan would have the same reaction.

"She seems okay to me."

"Tell you what. Take her home and see how she does. I'll have her back if it don't work out."

Dan sat at the kitchen table and wrote Delia a check that he tore off and laid on the table. Delia stirred with the spoon.

"Will you and Louise eat oyster stew?"

"You got extra."

"I always cook the same batch as when the kids were home. My grandpa used to make it in the winter. Us kids wouldn't get oysters, you had to be a certain age. We'd put the crackers in and let them swell up big as silver dollars."

Dan drove home with the new dog asleep on his lap and a mason jar of oyster stew on the floorboard.

Louise had never been to the house where Tiny and Joan Gower had lived. It was on a bend in the Boris road, from which no other houses could be seen. She got out of the Scout with the necklace in the box Tiny gave her at Mary's wake.

She knocked on the door and listened to the soft clatter of the wind chimes. "Look, someone has come to visit," they seemed to say. "Oh, it doesn't matter, doesn't matter . . ."

The chimes were made of sandalwood and, like the necklace, seemed an unusual item for Tiny to have laid eyes on, let alone acquired.

It was not too late to run until Tiny opened the door and raised his hand to cover his face. Louise pulled his hand away and saw the cuts and swelling.

"What the fuck happened to you?"

"Well, these guys come over, you know."

"No I don't. What guys?"

"There were four of them. Earl Kellogg. One of them Mansfields from Mixerton. I didn't know the other two. They were wearing their class rings."

"What was it about."

"I'm the Laughing Bandit."

"You have got to stop this shit, man."

"Well, that's what they said."

He went to the kitchen and came back with an ice pack made of a twisted washcloth and pressed it to his cheek.

She put the necklace box on the counter.

"I don't want this."

"You don't like it?"

"It's not a question if I like it. It isn't right."

"I thought who it would look good on, and you were the one that come to mind."

"Tiny . . ."

"You want to sit down? I'm kind of dizzy."

He went to the living room and settled into a chair with a leather back and wooden arms.

"You're married," said Tiny. "That's a given. But I just want to know something. With Micah gone, I've been thinking back. Would you've stayed with me if I'd done things different?"

Louise brought a kitchen chair over and sat looking at him, elbows on knees, the living room between them.

"I don't think so," she said. "It's been such a long time. You know. But I'd have to say, since you're asking, no. I don't think so."

"How come."

"At the time? I wanted what you stood for."

"What was that?"

"Trouble."

"Did I?"

"You want me to get a mirror?"

"And what were you to me?"

"I don't know."

"A way out," said Tiny. "Is what I think you were."

"Of what?"

"Everything. Myself. And fine-looking. To this day."

"Let's be quiet now."

He stood up. "I'm going to go lay down."

"Will you be all right?"

"Oh, yeah. I've had worse than this."

"Put something on those cuts."

"I've got rubbing alcohol. That'll probably hurt worse than the fight."

"And don't go after them."

"After what they did."

"You want to do things different, you make me that promise."

"All right. Promise."

Louise picked up the necklace and put it in her pocket. To do otherwise now would be to side with the gang that battered Tiny.

She went to him then and touched his face with her hand. "Take care of yourself," she said.

The woods were damp and sugary and mossy on the first weekend of May. Lyris and Albert walked the forest with backpacks. The birds flew tree to tree whistling broken songs.

They'd never camped together. It seemed like the next step for them as a couple.

"You think we'll find her," said Lyris.

"It's been, what, five months. Cops would have her if she was here."

"Tiny says they couldn't find cheap sandals at Target."

"You would question our heroes in blue."

"Every day I would."

"Well, you know, I got the map. Just seems like I ought to follow it."

They came to the river at the bottom of a ravine and followed it upstream. The river was twenty feet across with a rock wall on the far side and the current hurried along carrying dead branches and skeins of leaves plus the occasional beer can.

In late afternoon they found the abandoned fire ring of the Boy Scout camp opposite a rock ledge and narrow opening in the bluff.

"That's her tunnel," said Albert.

They dropped their packs on the ground and made camp. The tent had ridgepoles of shock-corded carbon and went up so fast and neatly they wished they had more tents to pitch.

Albert built a fire, opened a can of hash, and cooked it in a skillet. The sun went down as they ate, and shadows came over the campsite. Lyris took two bottles of beer from a cooler and passed one to Albert.

After supper they drank apple brandy and played cat and mouse with flashlights in the treetops. The tent was low and warm, and they crawled inside to go to sleep. The Twins were playing the Red Sox in Minneapolis, and they listened on the radio. The Twins were up 2 to 1 in the seventh. Lyris fell asleep with her head resting on Albert's arm, breathing with a tiny click in her throat.

Lyris cried out in her sleep. She'd dreamed that she was playing a parlor game, but no one would tell her the rules, and everything she said was stupid, and people laughed at her.

"That sounds like my regular day," said Albert. "Go back to sleep. Listen to the river."

"Shhh," she said, sitting up on her elbows. They heard soft steps. A shadow moved over the tent.

Albert pulled jeans on and picked up a flashlight and went out. He shone the light on the emaciated figure of Sandra Zulma. She hunkered by the fire ring, sifting coals with a hunting knife, hair long and matted around her face.

"Put that out," she said. "The moon's enough."

Albert turned off the flashlight.

"I wasn't expecting you," she said.

"Who were you expecting?"

"Do you have a message for me?"

"Have something to eat. That's my message."

"I don't do that."

"You don't eat."

"Nope."

"Maybe you should think about it."

She laid the knife on the ground and put sticks on the coals and leaned close to breathe on them, her body folded like a heron's. A circle of flames came up with a soft breath.

"Jack's coming," she said.

"Oh yeah?"

"He's meeting me here."

"That would surprise me."

"Who's your friend?"

"Her name is Lyris. We live together."

"How nice. Bring her out."

"What do you want?"

She turned toward him smiling with a pale and dirt-streaked face. There were pink scars on her forehead and the side of her face. "I'm not going to hurt you, Albert."

Lyris came out of the tent, a sleeping bag around her shoulders.

"Lyris Darling, this is Sandra Zulma," said Albert.

"Hi," said Lyris, her voice small and far away in the clearing, with the wraithlike Sandra building a fire.

"Don't be afraid," said Sandra.

"Well, I am. I am afraid."

"You have been a long time."

"How would you know?"

"I can tell."

"The knife isn't helping any."

Sandra sheathed the knife at her hip. "There. All better."

"Thank you."

The fire was going now. Sandra added kindling and then rested her upturned hands in the dirt in a strangely imploring gesture.

"This is certainly pleasant," she said.

"How did you get out of Stone City?" said Albert. "There were cops all over the place."

"A man gave me a ride. He gave me the knife. He gave me this."

She took the rock from her jacket and held it up, slate facets reflecting the firelight.

Albert thought of the things he might tell her. He'd been in her room, he'd seen her books, Jack Snow was dead. But he didn't know what she would do and wasn't eager to find out.

Sandra got up and stretched. "Well. I should be on my way. Jack will be looking for me."

"He's dead," said Lyris. "Don't you know that?"

"There's all kinds of dead," Sandra said. "Don't try to follow me. You wouldn't like it where I go."

"Come with us," said Lyris. "We'll take you home."

Sandra stood looking at the moon. Tears rolled down her face in silver tracks like beads of mercury. She wiped them away and stared at her hands.

"Take care of her, Albert. Don't forget her."

Sandra turned and walked to the river. She waded across in the moonlight, scrambled onto the ledge, and was gone. Lyris brought clothes from the tent. She dropped sneakers on the ground and hopped about pulling on jeans.

"Where are you going?" said Albert.

"After her."

"You heard what she said."

Lyris snapped her jeans with her chin on her chest. "She'll die. That'll be on us."

"We should call the cops."

"Oh my God."

"What do you think she meant?"

"About what?"

"She doesn't eat."

"It doesn't mean that."

"There's different kinds of dead."

"Ghosts don't carry knives," said Lyris. "They don't build fires."

"How do you know?"

"Come with me."

Albert followed Lyris into the river. The water swept cold around their legs. They climbed to the ledge, scraping hands and shins on the rocks. Sandra had had a much easier time of it. Albert shone the flashlight into the tunnel, the walls furred with moss.

"Sandra," called Lyris, her voice echoing down the passage.

They entered single file and holding hands. Albert fanned the flashlight on wings of bats like wet leaves pasted to the rocks. After they had gone a hundred paces, they began to hear the singing of many voices.

The tunnel angled left. Sandra held the knife and the rock, her eyes like blue glass.

"You can die if you want to," she said.

"Who is singing?"

"It's a radio."

Albert and Lyris returned to their camp, where they kept the fire burning all night. They didn't talk a lot but only passed the brandy back and forth or got up to fetch wood. They made love on the ground, gold and warm by the fire.

A park ranger arrived toward morning. He stepped into the clearing with uniform pants tucked into hiking boots in the old style. He had a broad neck and red face and brushy gray hair and mustache. The light was coming up over the bluff.

"I don't make a big deal of it," he said, "but you're supposed to camp in the numbered sites."

"We didn't know."

"It's posted."

"There was a woman here last night."

"What woman is that?"

"Do you know who Sandra Zulma is?"

"Everyone does," he said. "People see her sometimes. Think they do anyway. She's not here. She have anything to say?"

"Quite a bit."

"Sometimes she's just quiet."

"Look in the cave across the river," said Lyris.

The ranger laughed. "There ain't no cave across the river. That's just a story. You go in about ten feet and you hit solid rock."

"We were in it," said Albert.

The brandy bottle lay empty on the ground and the ranger shoved it with the side of his boot. "So you say."

"What the hell," Lyris said.

"This is a strange place," said the ranger. "I see lights sometimes, and they ain't campfires. My grandma used to talk about this fella had a cabin round here in the thirties. Baker. He would have parties in Prohibition and they'd hear the railroad men laughing in the trees. So then one day his friends come up to see what old Baker was up to and the cabin was gone and him with it. Like there hadn't been nothing there."

Louise put on black rubber boots with terra-cotta soles and walked the dog at dusk. They'd named her Pogo after a comic strip character Mary used to like. Louise and Pogo ambled past the barn, the dog swinging the bones of her shoulders and wagging her tail like a switch.

She hadn't turned out to be slow, though she did not like to be alone. The first nights they had her she would cry until Louise got up and lifted her into bed, where she burrowed slowly into the covers, exploring. She had slept at their feet ever since.

The path between the fields ran long and grassy under jet trails crossing and breaking in the sky. Louise threw a tennis ball for the

Lab, who sat rigid waiting for hands to clap before sprinting off and trotting back with the yellow ball in her grinning teeth. When they got tired of throwing and chasing the ball, they would walk side by side. The lane ended at a T intersection, where sometimes they went east, sometimes west, sometimes home.

CHAPTER SEVENTEEN

THE VOLLEYBALL players drank in a beach bar late at night. It was a dim tavern with a bicycle and mannequin and Christmas lights in a loft. One night Micah got drunk on tequila. You can have too much tequila and still seem all right for a while. Micah caught himself falling in the bar and borrowed a cell phone and went out in the night.

The road was empty and the asphalt seemed to turn around him. Safe on sand, he felt steadier and made his way to a lifeguard hut on pilings, and there he called Lyris.

"Hello?" she said.

"Sister," said Micah.

"Boy?"

"Yeah, hi."

"Where are you?"

"The Pacific Ocean."

"Do you know what time it is?"

Micah looked at his wrist. "I lost my watch. How is Albert?"

"He's good. Asleep."

"I'm going to find you. You're around here somewhere. Hold on. I'm checking."

"Micah, I'm home. Where is Joan?"

"On the seventeenth floor."

"Did she leave you?"

Micah climbed the ramp to the walkway that bordered the hut. He went all the way around looking for Lyris. "I live at the beach now. Listen. That's the ocean."

"What do you mean?"

"I was staying with Mark and Beth. These friends of mine. I've made so many friends, Lyris, you wouldn't believe."

"I'm glad."

"They have no idea who I am. But one night we were playing music and Mark didn't like the way Beth and I were dancing and he said I should leave. We were getting into it. The dancing, I mean. You can't blame Mark. So I've been sleeping on the beach and in the morning I go swimming and then I go back to sleep and then I play volleyball and that's what I do. Why aren't you here?"

"I'm in Stone City, Micah. You know that."

Micah descended the ramp and ducked through the piers. It was dark and cool under the stand. "I thought I could bring you here," he said. "By thinking of you. . . . I know that doesn't make sense."

"I'll come. Okay? Just give me a few days."

Micah crawled out and lay down in the sand and looked at the stars. The sand was good. "I'm kind of fucked up, Sister."

A vacuum cleaner followed Joan around the apartment, banging into her heels like a little red dog. She sprayed the surfaces with specialized cleaners that she suspected were all the same thing. Housekeeping was not her strong suit.

She put on sunglasses and took the elevator down to the lobby. The doorman stood in the shade of the awning in a forest-green coat with red epaulets.

"I'm going to run to the flower shop, Alexei," said Joan. "My daughter Lyris will be arriving any minute."

"Your daughter, yes. I remember."

"So, right, if she should get here, tell her she can go on up."

"Very good."

"On second thought, have her wait. The lobby's nicer, don't you think?"

"The lobby is a good choice."

"Maybe she should stand by the fountain."

"We don't tell them where to stand."

"Do you realize how long it's been since I've seen her?"

"Many years."

"I'm going to Larchmont to get some flowers. What kind of flowers would a young lady like?"

"Azaleas."

"What do they look like?"

"There are different varieties. Blue, yellow, orange. If I were a young lady an orange azalea would suit me very fine."

Lyris had yet to arrive when Joan got back. She arranged the azaleas casually as if she and Micah lived always among flowers. Ladybugs emerged from the petals and clung sleepily to the stems, then began bobbing around the apartment. They were picturesque at first but there were a lot of them.

Joan picked up a magazine and holding it open herded the ladybugs toward the windows as if there were something in the magazine she wanted them to read.

The intercom buzzed and Joan went and held the button down. Nothing said on the intercom could be understood in the apartment.

"Send her up," she said.

Joan opened the door and then went to the windows and pressed her thumbnails against her teeth.

"Hi, Joan," said Lyris.

Joan took a breath and turned to the door. Lyris wore a yellow sundress and faded jean jacket with threadbare elbows and frayed cuffs that people in this town would pay a fortune to have.

Joan crossed the room and took Lyris's hands in hers.

"You're so beautiful," said Joan.

"Where's Micah?"

"At the beach. He practically lives there."

"He told me he does live there."

"That's not true. He comes home sometimes."

"Joan, he's fifteen years old."

"I've made us lunch. You must be hungry from your plane ride."

"I want to see Micah."

Joan thought her knees would go out and she would fall on the floor. Lyris put her hand on her shoulder. "Okay, let's have lunch."

Joan went to the refrigerator and brought out sandwiches with radishes and cornichons, and they ate sitting at a table by the pullout couch where Joan slept.

"What's up with the ladybugs?" said Lyris.

"We have a lot of them in California."

"I knew you couldn't keep him."

"He's in Redondo, Lyris."

"I wanted to believe it would be all right."

"I know what you think. Joan is bad, Joan is a monster. Just wait till you see him. He's growing up."

"I can't reach him. I tried calling his number but it was somebody else's phone."

"Oh, he won't carry a cell phone. That's because of this club he was in at school."

People who look like they'll never win can be the most dangerous to play. You should ask yourself what are they doing here, what secret might they have.

Micah and a team player from Riverside were up against two brothers who sold furniture in Anaheim. In their thirties, they were not tall men but had arms and legs of particular density. They wore sand socks and Oakley shades. One had won a tournament at Mission Beach some year.

Ridges of hard sand broke underfoot. It was a hot day with a fair wind off the ocean. They were playing for twenty-seven dollars apiece because that was all Micah had on him.

The furniture dealers lost the first game but seemed to have used the loss to uncover the strength and weaknesses of Micah and his partner. Micah's sets varied in height and distance from the net. His teammate relied on a cross-court kill that could be anticipated and defended. Thus in the second and third games the brothers tried to make Micah set and his partner attack.

Plodding on in their methodical way, impassive behind their mirrored shades, the furniture brothers knew what they were doing, and their knowledge wore Micah down. He stood between points with hands on knees, breathing hard. Sand coated his arms and legs. He could feel his heart beating in the light and the trees and the water. He had never lost to anyone wearing sand socks.

The match came down to a serve that Micah hit long. It didn't break the way it was supposed to. The stocky brothers had outplayed them in an almost unbelievable way. "Ah well," thought Micah. He went to his sneakers and took out his last bills and paid the men from Anaheim. He could see a distorted image of himself in their glasses.

Then he heard someone call his name, and he turned to see Lyris and Joan standing in the shadow of three palm trees. He walked slowly toward them, dazed in the sun, as if they might be other people who looked like them. The lost match was all but forgotten. He hugged Lyris and lifted her off her feet, both of them laughing.

They walked down to the Pacific and she kicked off her sandals and they waded into the surf. Lyris's yellow dress floated on the water. A gull passed overhead, wings fixed, silent. A ship lay on the horizon like a city built on water. Micah and Lyris stood hand in hand, waves breaking against their legs, never falling back.

Acknowledgments

I would like to thank Elisabeth Schmitz, Sarah Chalfant, Brigid Hughes, and Paul Winner.

Author's Note

Though the recommended pronunciation of Cúchulaina varies, Sandra and Jack go with ku-HULL-in.